Produced by LouLou Productions LLC
Copyright © 2012 by David Carner
Cover design by R. Carner

Paperback ISBN: 978-0-9859514-7-4

To find out more about John Fowler, please feel free to follow my author page on Facebook. The David Carner fan page currently holds all announcements pertaining to this series. Also check out www.davidcarner.com for information on this series and any other works. You may also follow me on twitter @davidcarner.

The John Fowler Novels

The Road to Justice

Sins of the Son

This Thing of Ours

Journey's End

Day's Past (Coming Christmas 2014)

Check out http://david-carner.blogspot.com/ for my free short story, Bad Day in Queen's Landing. The blog is updated with a new chapter weekly.

Dedication

Warren, Ann, Charlotte, and Betty – Four people that forever shaped my life that aren't on earth, but are with me every day. Each of you made an impression on me that will always be remembered. I love each one of you, and wish you were still here.

Chapter 1

Dr. Brian Nichols sat down at the desk, exhausted. He had lost count of the amount of babies he had delivered in the past three days. He was behind on paperwork and knew he had to get caught up. He needed to call in one of the midwives, but they had delivered so many babies over the past month that he knew they needed rest. He knew Catherine would be at the clinic soon. It didn't matter how exhausted they all were; Catherine believed in the clinic and their mission. Brian looked at the clock and shook his head. Dealing with the Williams family and their new child had taken longer than he thought it would. For now, the couple was comfortable in their room. The baby was in the nursery with a camera feeding into a monitor in the couple's room. He needed to finish the death certificate for the hospital stillbirth three days ago. Brian still delivered babies at the hospital, but he was the director and consultant at the Birth Center here in Miami, Florida. He knew it was okay that it was late. His guy at the coroner's office would take care of everything, but he needed it done before Catherine arrived.

Outside the office, nine men and one female, all wearing presidential masks and armed, had gathered. Their leader, Felipe, didn't like the plan, but if what his cousin had told him was right, this was the best time to hit the clinic. They rushed the door, broke the glass, and entered. They knew they had tripped a silent alarm and only had minutes. They quickly found the doctor.

"Where's the baby!?" Felipe yelled, doing his best to disguise his voice. When the doctor wouldn't answer, the woman pushed a shotgun into Brian's face. He swallowed and led them to the child. The masked woman grabbed the child, looked it over, and held the baby close.

"There's nothing wrong with the baby," the doctor said quietly. The woman glared at him from behind the mask. The doctor couldn't see her, but he felt the glare full

4

of hate. They started back down the hall when Mark Williams stepped out of his wife's room.

"What's going on here?" he asked. He saw the baby. "Is this our child?"

"As far as you're concerned, this child was never yours," the woman in the mask said forcefully. "If you tell anyone what happened, especially the police, it will be the last thing you do. You can get another child; this one is no longer yours!" The man nodded. One of the masked men signaled with his gun for Mark to return to his room. Mark hurried to the room and shut the door. The group continued to the front door. Felipe held a gun to the doctor's head.

"You don't tell what happened here, and you'll never see us again, understand?" Felipe asked, again trying to disguise his voice. The group left in three SUVs.

Dr. Brian Nichols stood at the doorway. He had less than a minute to decide what to do before the police arrived. Mrs. Williams came running down the hallway.

"Where's my baby?" she cried. Before Dr. Nichols could calm her or console her, Catherine arrived. Brian knew there was now no choice but to tell the police that the baby had been kidnapped. He had never felt this scared in his life. He was told what would happen if the police were involved. He was sure he was a dead man walking.

6 Days Ago
Somewhere

Chapter 2

"John. John, you need to wake up."

John heard the voice clearly. He laid there with his eyes closed. All he could think about was how black it was. His mind was confused and muddled. He knew something was off, but he just couldn't put his finger on it. John knew he had to open his eyes, but he didn't want to. He also knew who the voice he had heard belonged to. How could he ever forget it?

"John, you've been shot," the voice said.

John slowly rubbed his hand across his chest, searching for the bullet hole that he had felt tear through him just minutes ago. There wasn't one, and that was strange, but not, all at the same time. He felt again and was surprised that there wasn't anything that felt wet or sticky. John thought he should feel panicked, but he didn't. He felt at peace.

"John," he thought to himself. "You don't need to be a great detective to figure this one out."

"JOHN EDWARD FOWLER!!!! You open your eyes this instant!!!" John knew of only two people who would ever yell at him like that, and the voice wasn't his mother's.

"Ok, Sam," John said, sighing. "I'll open them."

John opened his eyes. It was white all around, a bright, brilliant white. In the midst of all the white, he saw the figure he was looking for, Sam. Her hands were on her hips and she was staring at him, looking more than a little annoyed. John recognized that look. He had been the cause of that look many times.

"Are you mad because I told Jess I loved her?" John asked. He realized the absurdity of the question as soon as he said it. Sam was trying to look furious at him, but a smile broke across her face. She crossed the space between them and hugged John. Two conflicting thoughts crossed John's mind. One, if he could feel her, then he was probably dead. Two, he had Sam in his arms again, and that's all he cared about. Sam pulled away and looked John in the eye.

"You can't stay, John," Sam said with tears in her eyes. "You're not done with your work."

"I caught him, Sam, and I'm with you. Nothing else matters." Sam took John's hand and looked into his eyes.

"John, do you want Jess to go through what you went through?" Sam asked. John looked stunned. Sam continued. "She's loved you for a very long time, John, and honestly, you've loved her." Sam held her hand up before John could interject. "I know you love me, and I know you'd never cheat on me, but our time is over, John. It's time you chose her."

John crossed his arms and leaned back. He was sitting in a chair now. He really wasn't sure what was going on or where the chair had come from, but he wasn't leaving Sam. A look of annoyance crossed her face.

"Seriously?" she asked. "Seriously? We're gonna do this right now?"

"I've got nowhere else to be," John replied. Both of them realized what he said and began to laugh.

Cemetery
1 Day Ago

Chapter 3

Jessica Hammerstein looked out over the gravesite, saw all the umbrellas, and wished she had thought to bring hers. It was a dark and dreary spring day. Rain was lightly falling, but Jessica didn't really notice. Her face was wet from tears and rain. She wasn't really sure how she was supposed to feel. Today, the man she loved was having a funeral. Today, she had to watch a casket being dropped into the ground in the plot that belonged to Sam and John Fowler. John Fowler, the man she loved. It had taken a gunshot through his chest for her to realize how much he meant to her. She had known for a long time that she had cared for him, but this feeling . . . this was so much more.

Jessica looked at the headstone that had John's and Sam's names on it. Jessica shook her head at the irony; Sam had been her best friend. Sam had died over three years ago. Everyone thought Sam had died because of an explosion in Sam and John's apartment except for Jessica, Chet and Trip who had known the actual cause of Sam's death. John had just learned six days ago that Sam was killed by Bruce. Bruce had broken Sam's neck with his bare hands and used the explosion to destroy the evidence. Somehow, Bruce had survived the shot to the shoulder he had received at the hands of John and the three slugs Chet had put in Bruce after Bruce had shot John from behind. It wasn't fair. Bruce was lying in a hospital bed recovering, and all these people were gathered here for John's funeral. Jessica saw John's parents, and her stomach was in knots.

Jessica shook her head and looked up into the sky. The rain ran down her face. It had also just been six days since John looked Archibald Staples right in the eye and told him that he would see Archibald and his group of friends in jail if it was the last thing John ever did. Jessica thought that was the stupidest move John had ever made. Archibald was one of the most evil men in the world as far as Jessica was concerned. She was honestly surprised it had been Bruce that shot John and not Archibald or one of his flunkies.

Jessica looked across the graveyard and saw Archibald and his daughter standing there with smug looks on their faces. Jessica spoke.

"I have eyes on them," she said softly.

"Copy that. I have them on camera," replied a male voice. "Do you think they'll do anything?"

"I highly doubt it, Chet, but we owe this to John to watch their every move," Jessica replied.

Chet Morris was in the van. Jessica smiled when thinking about Chet. They had tried to have a relationship, but what they both had been after was information about John. It was now a running joke between them. Chet had been doing background checks on Archibald and Veronica for five days now. John was Chet's best friend, well, as good a friend as John would allow himself to have. Since the shooting, Chet had been looking everywhere electronically to find something on the two Staples.

The fact Chet couldn't find anything spoke volumes about the Staples. Chet was a computer savant. John always joked Chet could have been a millionaire computer programmer, hacker, or both. Jessica found herself thinking back to the conversation she and Chet had with Director Lionel Pennyworth Smothers III, known to everyone as Trip.

Chapter 4

Jessica walked into Trip's office where Chet was
already sitting. Jessica smiled to herself. So many in the
FBI thought Trip was a by the book director. In fact,
behind his back, many called him "By the book Lionel."
They would be stunned to learn the things Trip had done
over the past three and a half years. The director that never
stuck his neck out for anyone had done more questionable
things than Jessica knew was possible. Trip had
overlooked the fact that one of his agents was compromised
by a one-time loan shark who was now the head of a major
crime family. Trip had not reported a mole discovered
within the FBI a few weeks ago, so as not to alert the
higher ups who might be compromised by Archibald or
other members of his cabal. Trip had also used every trick
in the book to lure John back to the FBI for one simple
reason. The three people in this room felt they were
responsible for Sam's death and knew only John could
solve the case.

Sam had come to Trip before her death when she
thought she was being followed. Trip had gotten a New
York police undercover officer to watch John, thinking he
was the one in danger. In the end, it hadn't been John in
danger; it had been Sam. Sam had been watched and then
killed for the most idiotic reason Jessica had ever heard.

FBI agent Bruce Cosby had killed Sam Fowler
because he had thought she was his illegitimate half-sister.
Bruce's father, then Senator, soon-to-be Vice President
Jeremiah Cosby, had been gearing up for a presidential run
and was running on a family values platform among other
things. Bruce, fearing his father's name would be dragged

10

through the mud and for his job, since Bruce liked to throw his father's name around, killed Sam so no questions could be asked. Exactly how someone still couldn't have figured out Sam was the Senator's daughter since she was dead, Jessica still hadn't wrapped her head around. The easy answer to the whole mess was Bruce was stone cold crazy.

Jessica snapped back to the present. Trip looked grim.

"I've been given full authority," Trip began. He stopped a minute, choked up. He resumed quietly. "I've been given full authority to begin the task force on the Staples. We have it under good authority that they will be at John's funeral." Jessica smiled in spite of the situation. She knew the good authority was Jeremiah Cosby. She also knew that Trip had used the soon-to-be vice president to influence Quantico to okay the operation. Trip continued.

"We will need surveillance of them at the funeral, and then, you two are to go to Virginia to begin the investigation since that's the Staples' home base. A certain private individual has offered us the use of his home to conduct the investigation." Trip was grinning broadly. Jessica and Chet exchanged glances. Jessica smiled at Chet, but Chet still looked solemn. Jessica knew the individuals in question were the Moores, Sam's parents. Jessica was glad John had made up with them before the gunfight with Bruce. She knew the Moores would do everything in their power to help them bring down the Staples. Right now, Jessica's biggest worry was Chet. He spoke.

"Do you have . . ." Chet began. He gathered himself and continued. "Do you have any word on Bruce?"

Trip looked disgusted. "Yeah, he's gonna make it! You know, Chet, you should probably go back to the firing range and practice!" Jessica slammed her fist on Trip's

11

desk. Trip already regretted what he said. He began to apologize, but Jessica cut him off.

"Stop it!!" she exclaimed. "This bickering is not going to fix this situation we're all in." She crossed her arms over her chest. "I know we're all upset, but we've been here before. We can't fail John and Sam again! We have every reason to believe Archibald is behind The Duck rising to power. We have every reason to believe Archibald planted the idea in Bruce's head that Sam was Bruce's half-sister. We know he bought Chet's debt when he was gambling, and we know he tried to acquire my private student loan servicer. He's paid off loans on another four agents that we know of. And, then, there's this mysterious third person involved with Archibald and Duck. This guy is dirty, excuse me, these three are dirty, and we need to finish the job John started and bring them down."

Trip and Chet both looked ashamed of themselves. Trip reached his hand out to Chet. Chet took his hand and shook it. Jessica nodded and straightened her jacket.

"How is this going to work?" she asked. "The two of you and the Senator," she paused.

"That's just it," Trip interjected. "Jeremiah is about to be the Vice President of the United States, and he doesn't want his presence to stop Archibald from showing or make the funeral a bigger media circus than is already anticipated. He will have a private viewing and has already spoken to John's parents. As for Chet and myself, I have spoken to John's parents about us as well. They hope we catch Archibald doing something and are fine with us not being there. My excuse will be pressing Director's work, and Chet's will be he's beside himself with grief."

Jessica thought about the covers for a second, nodded, turned, and walked out of the office. After she left, Chet and Trip sat in silence for a minute. Chet broke the silence.

"Trip," Chet began. "Why the surveillance at the funeral?"

Trip leaned back in his chair. "You know Sam's dad, Arthur?" Trip asked. Chet nodded. "He believes Archibald is very likely to brag that he had something to do with convincing Bruce to kill Sam. Arthur believes he might brag about many things with John gone. It's worth a shot." Chet nodded. Trip continued. "You did the right thing with Bruce."

Chet held his head in his hands.

"Trip, if I had reacted quicker . . . " Chet began to sob. Trip got up, walked around his desk and put his hand on Chet's shoulder.

"I know, Chet, I know."

Cemetery
1 Day Ago

Chapter 5

Trip sat in the surveillance van and thought about the last four years. He could only think of one time things had gone worse than they did last week. It had to be the death of Sam Fowler and the reaction of John. Trip had pulled out the old case file a few days ago and looked it over. Given what happened, how could he not? He had his own personal notes on what had happened, things he never would have included in the official record. The lowest point may have been the interrogation of John by Jessica. Trip couldn't help but remember what had happened.

John had been taken into custody following the explosion of the apartment. He had been brought in directly from the street. He had changed out of his normal suit he wore with the FBI. Trip remembered that it had been one of the few times he had ever seen him that way, well, before that night. He had on a simple tee shirt, blue jeans, tennis shoes, and a jacket. He was still buzzing from earlier in the day. This was actually the second time he had been arrested that day. The first time he had been arrested along with several other members of the Mafia at This Thing of Ours Bar. It had been the most successful sting the New York FBI had in years. John had even tried to bribe the arresting officers, playing on the persona that he had gone rogue.

It had only been a few hours earlier that he had been the toast of the FBI. Everyone was smiling, even Bruce. Of course, Trip now knew that was because he had killed Sam and had rigged John's apartment to blow up. Trip shut his eyes as he drifted back to the memories of that day.

Chapter 6

John was sat down in a chair in the interrogation room. He turned and looked at the mirror that looked back at him. He had been almost a block away from the explosion, but it had knocked him down. No, that wasn't right; it had knocked him flat on his back. His head hurt from bouncing off the pavement. He noticed that the more the alcohol wore off, the more it hurt. Perhaps, he should have gone to the hospital. He probably would have if he cared if he lived or died.

John had been a part of too many deaths with his job in the FBI; he had known Sam was dead immediately when the apartment exploded. He had lain there for a minute, not sure what to do. He almost felt like his mind was broken. After a few minutes, he picked himself up and headed toward what was left of the apartment building. Sirens filled the air, and he knew in seconds he would be joined by firefighters. John was thinking about other victims. He had to. If he didn't, he'd walk right into the fire and never come out. As far as John knew, no one else had yet to rent an apartment in the newly renovated building, but John had to be sure. He tried to make his way inside the structure, but before he could, hands grabbed him and dragged him away. He didn't even have it in him to fight to go inside.

Earlier, everyone had encouraged him to call Sam and have her come down and get him after the party, but John wanted nothing to do with the FBI right now. He was considering resigning before all of this had happened. In fact, he was going to tell Sam that if she wanted him to quit, he would. John noticed he was being given oxygen.

He was confused. He knew he hadn't been sitting there that long, but there were people everywhere. He heard voices that he recognized. After a few seconds, he realized it was Jessica and Trip. There was no doubt in his mind. John just sat and listened. They were arguing over questioning someone. John must have hit his head harder than he thought. Jessica sounded like she didn't want to question someone. Jessica loved to interrogate people the way most men loved watching football.

John looked around. He noticed several officers around him, all watching him while trying not to. John may have been drunk as a lord, but he knew exactly what was going on. John was being considered a suspect. He waved one of the officers over to him.

"Read me my rights," he said. The police officer looked confused. "Read me my rights, so I can admit my part in my wife's death, and we can make it all legal."

Chapter 7

John chuckled to himself. The move of admitting his guilt had caused Jessica and Trip all sorts of problems, but John really didn't care. Sam was dead, and he just didn't care anymore. Worse yet, it was all his fault, well not in the traditional sense. He hadn't physically killed her, but he had talked to a bartender about the case and her a few nights ago, and he knew it was his chatting that had led to her death. Emotion gripped John, and he didn't even try to fight it. He welcomed the feeling. It was the first real feeling he had in months. It was the first feeling he had allowed himself since Mark's death. Mark Glass had been undercover for months before John was. Some time ago (John had lost track when) Mark was killed, and John was forced to cover it up to prove he was a mole in the FBI. John did, but it almost killed him. John began to drink more than ever since Mark's death. It was the only way to kill the pain he felt.

John began to sob uncontrollably. He didn't care who was watching on the other side of the glass. He didn't care if he spent the rest of his life in jail. It was obvious it was his fault Sam died. He had a moment of weakness the night before and told the bartender everything, and now, Sam was dead because of it. There was no question in John's mind. He didn't care what happened to him, but he did care they were treating him like a common criminal. That was fine with him if that's what they wanted. John jumped up, grabbed the chair he was sitting in, and flung it at the glass.

"Send her in!!" he screamed as the chair bounced off the glass. He heard people scrambling out in the halls. John picked his chair up, chuckling to himself. If he was going to have to go through this ordeal, then he hoped to make all of the rest of them as uncomfortable as he was.

The door flew open, and Jessica stood there.

"I'm sorry, Precious. Was I interrupting your manicure?" John slurred. Jessica was the best interrogator in the FBI. She was also possibly the most attractive agent John had ever laid eyes on. Everyone in the FBI feared to be in an interrogation room with her. She could work people in the box like no one John had ever seen. John thought he would do everyone a favor and just admit what happened. And, for the first three hours of the interrogation, that's exactly what he did.

Chapter 8

"How is he?" Trip asked Jessica. John had been interrogated on and off for the past six hours. He constantly declined a lawyer. He kept saying it was his fault Sam was dead but wouldn't tell why. That's when Jessica went to work. She found out about a bartender at the This Thing of Ours Bar that John had talked to. The problem was John didn't know what he had told the bartender.

"He's sobering up," Jessica offered. She was seated at a table with the file on Sam's murder in front of her. At this point, they knew that Sam's neck had been broken before the explosion killed her. Trip harrumphed and handed her a cup of coffee. "He keeps asking for gin," she added.

"Gin?" Trip asked. Jessica gave her own grimace and nodded. "The bartender is the undercover agent we put on John to tail him," Trip said. "I've talked to him and forwarded everything to the director. He's been cleared."

"The Director of the FBI?" Jessica asked, surprised. Trip nodded.

"An agent's wife was killed. That gets the director's attention," Trip replied. "The director says give it another hour or two, and if you can't find anything, we can clear John."

"Sir," Jessica began in protest. "He has lost his wife. He lost Mark and had to cover it up. He's on the breaking point. He thinks all of these deaths are his fault, and he's ready to pay for something he didn't do. I know he's a pain, but no one deserves this."

"You're 100% right, Agent Hammerstein," Trip replied. "No one deserves this, but we have to be beyond sure." Trip paused. "The three of us make this our number one priority going forward. We find out who killed John's wife. Are we clear?" Jessica smiled into her coffee cup. "I figured I didn't have to tell you but just in case."

"Did Chet find anything at all?" Jessica asked. Trip shook his head.

"He's asleep in my office," Trip replied. Jessica laughed. Trip smiled. "He's been digging as hard as he can, but there's nothing. John's bank accounts are clear, and Chet can't find anything that would suggest a hit among the known Mafia hitmen. Plus, everyone that would have carried out something like this is in jail except for this mysterious man that John was talking about a few weeks ago. Goose, no, that's not it. Duck! That's the name, Duck." Jessica nodded. She glanced through the file one last time, and then began to rise. When she stood, she stopped and looked at Trip.

"I know why you had them run that pregnancy test on Sam, but what are we going to do if it comes back positive?" Jessica asked. "I'm not for sure what I'm hoping to happen if it was to come back positive. Do we want it to be John's, or to be someone else's? Either answer will kill John."

"You let me worry about that," Trip replied. Jessica nodded and walked away. What Trip didn't tell Jessica was he already had the results of the test. Sam was pregnant, and it was John's child. Neither person in the box needed that information right now. At some point, Trip would have to decide if he would tell anyone or not, but not right now.

Chapter 9

Jessica took a deep breath and prepared herself to enter the box. This was killing her. She and Sam had become best friends in the past few months. Making things even harder was Sam knew that Jessica was crazy about John. Why did she have to care for that man? John Fowler was conceited, obnoxious, childish, and he knew he was one of the best in the FBI. Yet at the same time, he was charming and charismatic in his own way, and there was something about his beliefs and values that were so old-fashioned. But, at the same time, it struck something in her. Jessica had always known there was nothing for her and John. Sam used to kid Jessica that if something happened to Sam then Jessica better bolt herself in her home because she was going to go after him.

Jessica shook her head, trying to rid herself of the thoughts. She wanted to cry. She had lost Sam, and John was a broken mess. What worried Jessica even more was what John was going to do once he sobered up. Jessica steadied herself and opened the door. John was lying with his face on the table while sitting in the chair. Jessica wanted to get him a pillow and a blanket, but she couldn't, and she knew it.

"John," she said loudly. "John, wake up. We need to talk again."

"Will you just arrest me?" John mumbled into the table.

"I need to know what happened tonight, John," Jessica replied.

"I've told you over and over and over and over and over," John replied, face still on the table.

"Then, tell me again," she said, more sternly.

"Sam died. Blew up. Blewwey." John was muttering into the table still. Jessica thought John wasn't quite as drunk as he was still acting. By her count, he hadn't had a drink in over eight hours. She wondered if it was a defense mechanism. She wanted to comfort him and tell him everything would be okay, but she knew this is what she could do for him. She could clear him, and then, he could begin to pick up the pieces of his life. Hopefully, when that time came, she would still be in it. She shook her head again, trying to drive the thoughts from her head.

"John," she began again. "Why were you there?"

"I live there, Miss Detective," John replied. "I know you love ripping the hearts and souls from people in this room, but you can't rip mine out, Jess. You know why? Because mine's gone! My soul was ripped out when I covered up Mark's death, and my heart was ripped out when they killed my wife. Now, please put me in jail for the murder of my wife!"

Chapter 10

"John," Jessica began, fearing his wrath. "Do you want a lawyer?" John sat up and then sprang up from his chair and began to pace. Jessica let him go and signaled to the people in the other room to leave him alone.

"Why would I want a lawyer?" John demanded. "Do you know what a lawyer would say? He or she would say it's not my fault. I DON'T CARE WHAT THEY THINK!!!" Do you understand me!?! It's my fault she's dead!! I talked!! I talked last night at that bar to that bartender Ricardo something or other! He had her killed. It's my fault she's dead!" John was beside himself.

"John," she responded calmly. "We talked to him. He's clean, John. It wasn't him." John slapped the table and leaned in close.

"Then it's all my fault!" John responded. Jessica tried to stop him, but he cut her off. "Shut up for a minute! I know this is your special place, but shut up and listen. I'm a drunk! I'm a drunk, and I talked! I killed her! I didn't personally do it, but it's my fault, and you need to lock me up! Please, Jess," John was begging with tears in his eyes. "Lock me up, and throw away the key. I don't deserve to be free for what I did. I talked, and she died, and I can't live without her!" Jessica wanted to stop this and go hold him, but she couldn't. She had to stay strong for John and for Sam. Sam would never forgive her for not clearing John. She plowed ahead.

"Did you physically kill your wife?" she asked as she braced for the verbal assault.

"NO!!!" John screamed. "What kind of sick creep do you think I am!?! I would never hurt her! I love her!" John stopped, his face racked with pain. He whispered. "I loved her." He paused for a few seconds. Trip was watching the whole thing ready to end it, but he caught Jessica slightly shake her head no. She wanted him completely cleared. John continued.

23

"What about Duck?" he asked. "What about him?"

"There is no sign of Duck," Jessica responded. "Walk me through it one more time," she gently urged. John sighed.

"For the fifth time, Jess, I was heading home," he began. "The case was over, the party was over, and I was going home. Have I told you what I was going to do when I got there? I was going to tell Sam I was entering rehab. I was gonna resign, Jess. If she asked me to, I was going to resign." Jessica hated herself for what she was going to ask next.

"John," she began. "Are you sure you hadn't already been home? John, you were drunk. Are you absolutely sure you hadn't been home and the explosion went off after you left your house?" John exploded.

"JESS, I DIDN'T KILL MY WIFE WITH MY OWN HANDS!! I didn't! I may have told someone something that led to her death, but I didn't do it! I didn't set the bomb that killed her. I didn't." John's voice trailed away as emotion ran through him. Trip had had enough and went to the interrogation room door. Jessica had gone over every possible scenario. They had found a witness that had seen John approaching the apartment, but the director had said to make sure. Trip was sure. He knocked on the door, and when it opened, he told Jessica to end it. She turned toward John.

"John," she began with a smile. "You're free to go. We have a witness that said he saw you approaching your house and not leaving it. For now, we'll need to keep your badge and gun, but you're free." Jessica was considering hugging him. She thought maybe she should offer to drive him home. All of those thoughts quickly went out the window.

"Did you get your pound of flesh?" John asked, sneering at Jessica. He walked past her and stopped in front of Trip. His voice was very quiet, but intense. "You

24

know what? Keep the gun, and keep the badge because I QUIT! You hear me, Lionel? I QUIT!"

Cemetery
1 Day Ago

Chapter 11

Brother Noble Cobb stood over John's casket. John
had told his parents years ago should something ever
happen to him, he wanted his boyhood pastor to preach his
funeral. There were tears in Bro. Cobb's eyes, but he held
them back and began to speak, his voice carrying over the
graveyard.

"I won't speak long," Bro. Cobb began. John's
father, Henry, gave Noble a smile, which Noble returned.
Noble had already spoken at the church for friends and
family. The gravesite was more for colleagues and agents.
"There's a popular song right now that uses the lyrics,
'What do I stand for?' You never had to ask that question
of our fallen friend here today. You knew exactly what
John Fowler stood for; justice. I've heard all the stories of
what happened after his wife's death and how he dealt with
it. Not being able to bring the man that killed former agent
Mark Glass to justice nearly killed John."

Noble paused and looked around. Archibald looked
slightly uncomfortable. Noble knew it shouldn't, but deep
inside, it pleased him. He continued.

"Some people over the years have said John's
ability has caused him to have problems, socially. I counter
that argument. You always knew where you stood with
John Fowler. You knew what John stood for, and you
knew what he would do for justice. John didn't care what
you believed, what your preference was in anything. John
didn't care about your sex, social standing in life, or if you
could do him a favor one day. John was dedicated to clean
up crime, corruption, and injustice. Today is the proof of
dedication. Yes, he paid the ultimate sacrifice, but would

any of you expect anything less of him?" Noble let the question hang in the air. He continued softly. "Would each of you do the same? Would you make the ultimate sacrifice for justice?" Many of the agents nodded, but some, some were clearly uncomfortable. Jessica was glad there were cameras everywhere. Some agents were going to find themselves answering some serious questions in the days to come, but that was for later. Noble continued.

"So, let me end with this thought. Today, we should celebrate. We celebrate the life of John Fowler, and we can all hope that one day when we end up here because it is inevitable, that someone can say the same thing about us."

The ceremony at the gravesite ended, and Jessica snapped back to her duties. She searched for the Staples and finally saw them. Her stomach sank. Archibald and Veronica saw Jessica and waved with an evil smile on both of their faces. They then began to head toward John's parents. There was no way Jessica was going to allow that to happen. It was bad enough the Fowlers were at their son's funeral, but Jessica was not about to let Archibald get in his famous digs. Jessica made long strides across the ground. She moved as quickly as she could in the soggy ground, but not fast enough. She arrived just a second behind the Staples.

Archibald extended his hand toward Henry Fowler, John's father. Henry and John had given each other nicknames when John was younger. John and Henry had been waiting for a college basketball game to start one Saturday morning when John was a teenager. While they were waiting, there were cartoons on the channel the basketball game was scheduled to come on. During the cartoons, the characters had called each other George and Bubba. By the time that day was over, Henry was George, and John was Bubba. Jessica had heard John refer to his father as George so often, she had slipped and called him that when they met a few days ago. Henry told her she could call him George anytime she wanted to.

Jessica was determined that Archibald was not going to talk to the Fowlers; unfortunately for Jessica, Veronica was determined her father would and stepped in front of her. Henry took Archibald's hand but didn't shake it. He held it still.

"Are you Archibald Staples?" Henry asked. Archibald nodded and looked down at his hand. "Look me in the eye," Henry demanded. Archibald snapped his head up, not used to being talked to that way. "Shut your mouth before you swallow a fly. My son told me about you. You know the one thing I hate the most about his death? He didn't get a chance to put you or your murderous daughter in jail." Archibald looked like he had been slapped. John's mother, Edna, had been staring at the coffin with tears flowing down her cheeks. She looked up at Archibald with daggers in her eyes. Archibald caught the look. In all of Archibald's dealings with crime lords and other criminals, he had never seen such a look of anger as he saw at that moment.

"I would like for you," Edna said, pointing at Archibald, "And your daughter, to leave right this instant! If you do not, I will have Jessica arrest you for physically terrorizing me and my husband!"

"Lady, there is no such thing!" Archibald exclaimed, still trying to get his hand away from Henry.

"I'm sure I can come up with some reason to hold you," replied Jessica. Henry threw down Archibald's hand in disgust. Archibald and Veronica turned to leave. Archibald couldn't help himself and spun around.

"You two old fools! Your son and his wife died because some insane nut thought Sam was his half-sister. I am sorry I ever suggested such a thing to Bruce, but if you think that is enough to arrest me, you are a fool!!!"

Archibald was beet red. Edna calmly walked up to Archibald.

"Do you care what anyone thinks of you, sir?" Edna asked. Archibald scoffed. "I'll take that as a no. I am going to do the hardest thing I've ever had to do. I am going to forgive you." Archibald scoffed again. "Mr. Staples, you don't understand. You caused the death of my daughter-in-law, Samantha. Then, my son tracked down her killer which leads us to today. You're an evil man, but I have to forgive you. If I don't, it will eat me alive. I won't give you the satisfaction of hurting anyone else in my family. I forgive you, Mr. Staples, but you need to ask for forgiveness. You need to ask for forgiveness for all the people you've hurt and lies you've told and crimes you committed!!"

Edna was shaking from the emotional outpour. Henry gently pulled Edna away, and they walked back to their waiting car. Jessica stared daggers at Archibald.

"You basically give a nut the reason he needs to kill her son, and she forgives you?" Jessica asked, seething. "You don't deserve to be around her, Archibald. Leave."

"Those two in the ground got exactly what they deserved!" Archibald spat at Jessica. Archibald then turned and began to leave with Veronica following behind him. Jessica watched Archibald and Veronica walk away. Archibald stopped at his vehicle and stared over at the Fowlers' car. He shook his head and got in the car. Jessica heard her earpiece crackle.

"Jessica," said Trip. He was in the van with Chet. "You do realize that by allowing both parties to separate and throwing the Staples out of the graveyard, you ruined any chance of getting Archibald to admit to anything, right?"

"I understand," Jessica replied.

"Good job, Agent Hammerstein. I think John would appreciate what you did. His mother is a better person than I could ever hope to be."

Jessica nodded, unable to speak. She looked up at the sky as the rain continued. She hated this. Arthur Moore walked up to Jessica to ask her how she was. Before he could say a word, she began to cry. Arthur held Jessica while she wept. In the truck, Chet and Trip turned off the listening device. Trip looked out the window at the rain and wondered if there wasn't another way.

Somewhere
6 Days Ago

Chapter 12

"I know all about the baby, Sam. I know about both of them. I know that you lost a child before we met, and I know that you were pregnant when you died. There's something I need you to know; I'm sorry. I'm sorry I didn't realize you were pregnant, and I'm sorry I never knew about the first child. Why couldn't you tell me about the first child, Amanda?" John asked. Sam just smiled.

"She's the key," Sam said. John was confused by her answer, but he was even more confused by the look on her face. Sam was staring at John. John was starting to feel a pain in his chest. He looked down, and blood was starting to flow down the white tee shirt he was wearing. He looked up at Sam; concern covered her face.

"John," Sam began. "Listen to me. You're not dead, yet. This isn't heaven or wherever you think it is. This is your mind, John. Do you understand me, John?"

John was starting to feel pain spreading all over his body, radiating from the hole in his chest. It dawned on him that he was bleeding very quickly. He had to stop it. Sam was on one knee in front of him. She put a finger on his lips. She smiled at him; her eyes were beginning to tear up.

"Listen to me," Sam said. "You have to go back. It's not time for us to be back together again. John, listen to me. Don't do to Jessica what I did to you. Do you understand me? I didn't have a choice, but you do. You have to choose her over me this time. John, if you don't, you're dead!"

John suddenly saw sparks everywhere. The whiteness and Sam disappeared for a second. He realized his eyes were closed. He tried to open them. As they barely opened, he saw a man over him with shock paddles. Behind him was Jessica, crying. Suddenly, he was in the white room again. Sam was there again, looking very irritated.

"John!!" Sam yelled. "You can't stay!!"

"I miss you, Sam," John said. He felt all of his strength leaving him. "I miss you." He reached up and took her hand. Sam held his hand against her face. She smiled at him.

"It's time to choose, John. You need her, and you need to live. I'll miss you, but our time is over. I love you both. Good-bye, John." The room sparked again. John didn't try to open his eyes. He heard a voice. It was Jessica.

"John, don't you dare leave me!! John!! John, I love you!!"

The room fluttered between reality and the whiteness. John knew he had to make a decision. He finally had to choose between Jessica and Sam.

Chapter 13

Jessica threw the television remote across the room. Her favorite fighter in MMA had just lost a match because, for some reason, he had tried a spinning back-fist. Why had a ground and pound technician used a spinning back-fist, she had no idea. She stood up, stretched, and went to retrieve the remote. She knew she wasn't just mad at the match. She was mad about having to watch John's parents lay him to rest. It just wasn't right. John was their only son, and in less than four years, the Fowlers had had to bury both Sam and John. Jessica shook her head. She knew she needed to get to bed, but she didn't want to.

"Sam," she said softly and looked around. She didn't see her friend anywhere. Not that she should, it's just Sam had been showing up several times over the past few weeks to both Jessica and John. Jessica knew it was their minds messing with them. No, she didn't know that. She sat back down on the couch. "I really need to talk," she said and looked around again. She was still alone. Jessica closed her eyes and tried to drift off to sleep.

She couldn't, as much as she tried. What she did do was remember the last funeral she attended with John's parents, Sam's funeral. Her mind took her back to that similarly rainy day almost four years ago.

Cemetery
Then

Chapter 14

Rain drizzled from the sky as John tried his best to hide the flask in his interior pocket of his coat. He had been drinking all of his waking hours since leaving the FBI. John knew Sam would be disappointed in him, but right now, he didn't care. Sam wasn't here and never would be again. There was nothing John could do to change that. The only way he would see her again was if he was to die, and right now, that thought wasn't so bad.

John had managed to avoid his parents and Sam's parents for the majority of the funeral, but now, here in the cemetery, he was cornered. No matter which way he went, he was going to run into them. He decided on the lesser of the two evils and chose his parents. He spoke to them for several minutes, but he couldn't begin to tell anyone what he said to them. He knew he said something about it being God's fault Sam was dead, and his mother admonished him. He knew the look of disappointment his father gave him as his dad led his mother away from John. He stood and watched them leave as he took a draw from the flask. As he screwed the top back on, he heard another voice calling to him, one he did not want to hear.

"John," Arthur called out. "What are you doing?"

"Trying to join Sam, if you really must know, Arthur," John replied, not turning to look at him. John knew that Arthur and Madeline hated him and blamed him for the death of their daughter.

Madeline and Arthur watched John. They were both concerned about John. He hadn't taken Sam's death well at all, not that anyone would, but John was reaching new depths with his drinking. No one wanted to get too close to him for fear that he would lash out at them. That, and he smelled like a gin distillery.

"John," Arthur began.

"Arthur, leave it alone!" John said quietly. He stood there a second and then spun to face him. "You have to stick your nose into every little thing I do, don't you?"

"John," Arthur began, trying to keep him calm. "I'm sorry if I ask about your job. I'm just curious as to what you do."

"More like checking up on your good for nothing son-in-law that's not good enough for your daughter!" John spat. "Well, it's your lucky day. I'm going to do what you always wanted. I'm getting out of your life forever!" With that, John walked away. Arthur and Madeline looked stunned. Jessica had seen the whole exchange and walked up to them.

"You know he's not in his right mind?" she asked. They both nodded. Jessica watched John storm off as best as he could. He weaved through the cemetery. Jessica had to stifle a laugh when he tripped over a tombstone, nearly fell, righted himself, and then proceeded to chew it out. She turned to the Moores. "You know, in his mind, you probably cussed him out, and he was striking back for something that only he knows about."

"He was saying I'm interfering in his life," Arthur said, still stunned. Jessica shook her head. "He needs to solve this murder, Jessica. It's the only way he'll move on." Jessica nodded.

"I know, Arthur, but he's not ready," she replied. Arthur nodded reluctantly.

"When he is, I'm going to be there," Arthur began. "I'm going to push him until he does. If he doesn't solve it, it will eat him up inside." Arthur looked sadly at Jessica. "Sam told me that cases can eat him alive. That's part of what was wrong with him. Something happened in that Mafia case that drove him to drink." Jessica crossed her arms and looked over the cemetery watching John weave and bob through headstones.

"That would make a lot of sense," Jessica replied, looking back at Arthur. "I don't know what all happened, but something changed him." The three watched John continue on across the cemetery in silence.

Chapter 15

Jessica pulled the car up in front of the Moore home. Chet sat beside her. He had been very quiet on the drive. Jessica turned toward him. She had asked Chet a question on the drive to the Moores' and Chet had no idea how to answer her.

"Chet," Jessica began. "Let's forget what I said." Chet nodded. That was the best thing he had heard today. Jessica got out of the car and walked up to the Moores'. She rang the doorbell, and Madeline opened the door. She hugged Jessica and walked inside with her. They walked through the house and stood in the doorway of a bedroom.

"How's he been?" Jessica asked.

"Do you remember the book about the little boy that wanted to attend his own funeral?" Madeline asked. Jessica smiled and nodded. "He really wanted to go."

Jessica smacked her palm on her forehead. She started shaking her head and began laughing.

"Doesn't every boy want to see his own funeral?" a familiar voice asked.

Jessica never even raised her head. "John, you're not a boy. You're an adult." Jessica looked up and saw John lying in bed. He had monitors attached to him, and an older nurse was sitting in the corner, reading a magazine. She was the private nurse the Moores had hired. John had a big grin on his face.

"I'm a kid at heart," John answered. "Are you here to help me bathe? I can't keep Lindsey's hands off me over there." The nurse stopped flicking through her magazine at mid-flick and glanced at John. She gave a "hrmph" and went back to what she was doing. Jessica covered her mouth with her hand, so John couldn't see her laughing.

The bullet wound had been a through and through. It was at the hospital, after John had been shot, that Chet had come up with the idea to fake John's death. Chet believed Archibald would not be as worried about the FBI if he believed John died, and frankly, after the things John had said to Archibald, John might be safer if Archibald thought John was dead. Arthur Moore had gotten there right as Chet had been describing the plan to Trip. Arthur offered the use of his home for John to recover but warned them of what this might do to the Fowlers.

Trip approved the plan to protect John and his family. Trip had been in on the plan for John to try and upset Archibald the day before, but he had no idea about John threating Archibald. Trip was now very concerned about John's well-being.

"Do you two realize what Archibald might do to John?" Trip admonished Chet and Jessica. "That idiot in there shot a gun right in Archibald's face! Archibald could take that as a threat to his manhood or something stupid like that! Chet, you said yourself that he's an alpha male!" Chet nodded like a child being scolded. Jessica looked Trip right in the eye and answered him with a straight face.

"You're just mad you didn't see John push Archibald over the edge," she replied.

"You're right, I am!" Trip answered, a smile forming, undermining his ability to chew out his agents. "Do you think anyone has ever stood up to Archibald like that before?"

"No," Jessica replied. "No one I know has the intestinal fortitude to do what he did." Jessica paused and then continued. "Well, it could have just been stupidity, but no one has the amount of whichever one it takes to do what he did."

"He's going to be ok," Trip said quietly. "John is going to be ok."

"No, he's not," Jessica answered. "Because I'm going to kill him for putting me through all of this."

Chapter 16

John studied Jessica's face. He didn't need to have his ability to read people to see what she was thinking about. Honestly, a blind man could see what she was thinking about. John decided to proceed carefully.

"You said in the hospital that we were going to have a," John used finger quotes, "'come to Jesus meeting' when I was better. Am I better enough now?" John looked a little nervous. Jessica smiled at him. There was love in the smile. John could see it, but there was something else, and John didn't know what it was. That was John's biggest problem with his gift; he had trouble when it came to the opposite sex and himself. He just couldn't read what was going on.

"It's not just going to be one meeting," Jessica replied quietly. John winced. "You faking pain won't get you out of them, either," she added.

"I'm sorry I went without you to confront Bruce," John said.

"I know," Jessica replied.

"Not good enough?" John asked.

"No," Jessica replied simply. John could see she was starting to get a little worked up and figured a tirade was coming. Apparently, Lindsey did too because she left. As she went through the door, she gave John a smile. It was somewhat sick and sadistic, and it made John shiver. Jessica walked over, grabbed John by the jaw, and turned his head to where he was staring directly into her eyes.

"You better listen good, mister," she said, barely above a whisper. "You are going to pay for what you pulled. I was worried sick, and don't give me any of those fake crocodile tears of you worried about us breaking up. I'm sticking with you until you learn your lesson on this one. Do you understand me?" John nodded his head, Jessica's hand still holding his jaw.

"And furthermore," she continued. She leaned in with her lips less than an inch from his. "If you ever pull a stunt like this again, I am going to kill you, so you don't have to choose between me and Sam. Are we clear?" John swallowed and nodded. Jessica gave him a quick peck on the lips and then held his face for a few seconds longer. She let go, and John let out a breath. He hadn't even been aware he had been holding his breath. He rubbed his jaw and looked at Jessica.

"What do you mean choose between you and Sam?" John asked. Jessica looked surprised just for a split second. She hadn't meant to mention that. She tried to recover by waving one of her hands as if to wave away the question. She began to walk back around the bed and back to the door. "Did you hear?" he asked very quietly. Jessica stopped and never turned around.

"Get some rest, John," she replied, still facing forward, with tears in her eyes. "We'll talk later." She walked out of the room. John lay in bed, remembering what he could of what happened after he was shot.

Somewhere
6 Days Ago

Chapter 17

The white room was gone, and it was very, very black around John. He knew his chest hurt. He forced his eyes open. There were hands all around him, but there was one face he could see. Jessica. The look on her face was indescribable, but if John was forced to describe it, it was the look he had on his face when he realized that Sam was dead from the explosion. John closed his eyes, and the past few weeks with Jessica ran through his thoughts. They had been amazing. Then, Sam made her way into his thoughts. She was smiling at him. John knew it was time to make a choice.

"You're right, Sam," he said very weakly. Why was he so weak? He pressed on. "Our time is over. I love her, Sam. I love her." John was just so tired. It seemed to be getting very black, and then, it wasn't. He swore he saw blue, white, and orange. Another charge had shot it's way though his body. He found he suddenly had the strength to scream, and scream he did. He gathered every ounce of strength he had left. "I love Jessica, Sam! I love her, and I'm staying with her! I choose Jessica!"

He felt a hand grab his. John's eyes opened, and there were all the hands working on him, but he only saw one face. He saw the tear-stained face of Jessica. John knew he didn't read emotions like love well, but that's what he saw on her face. He gathered his strength one last time.

"I choose you, Jess. I love you." John felt like he had run ten miles. He didn't remember much for the next few days, but each time he felt like he was waking up, he felt a hand in his, or a hand running up his arm, or a head lying on his shoulder. He knew it was Jessica. He also knew that Sam was gone. Whatever she was, a ghost, an angel, or his and Jessica's subconscious; Sam was gone. For the first time since her death, he didn't feel guilty for not thinking about her, or for thinking about Jessica instead of her. John had finally moved on, and he had made the conscious choice to do so.

Moore Home, Virginia
Hours before Kidnapping at the Birth Center

Chapter 18

John lay in bed for a few seconds and decided he had had enough. He grabbed the covers and flung them off him. He grabbed the rolling heart monitor and IV bag and tried to stand. He immediately stopped. He didn't realize how much this was going to hurt. He looked around to make sure he wasn't bleeding. He also double-checked to make sure he was covered in the back. He began to get up again. After that small battle was over, he realized he was going to have to walk. He took a deep breath and took a step, then another, and then another. After what seemed to be about an hour and a half, he made it to the door. He was nearly drenched in sweat, but he was determined. He stuck his head through the door and saw Jessica leaning against the hallway wall, looking up at the ceiling.

"For the love of God, don't move!" he yelled at Jessica. At least, he thought he yelled. He didn't know how much air he had left as hard as he was breathing from walking across the floor. Jessica closed her eyes, not believing what she thought was going on down the hall. She opened them and looked down to the doorway of John's room, and there was Captain Dodo making his way down the hall, albeit very slowly. She was really considering hurting him.

"What do you think you're doing!?" she bellowed as she pushed herself off the wall and started down the hallway towards him. Arthur and Madeline came to see what the yelling was about. When they saw, they stopped, looked, and smiled at each other and stood back to watch the show.

"Running a marathon," John answered testily. "What does it look like I'm doing?"

"Besides being stupid?" Jessica replied just as testily. "You could hurt yourself!"

"That implies that me doing this doesn't hurt," he retorted through gritted teeth. Madeline leaned in to Arthur after this exchange.

"Could he hurt himself?" Madeline asked quietly. Arthur shook his head.

"No, the doctor has been wanting him to get up and get around," he answered. Madeline smiled and went back to watching the show developing in front of them.

"Why would you come out here after me?" Jessica asked. She was slowing her walk, make him come to her. John looked amazed.

"Well, I came back from death for you. Seems like a walk down the hall isn't that big of a deal," John replied. Jessica stopped and stared daggers at him.

"Oh," she began, putting her hands on her hips and glaring at him. "You're playing that card?"

"You only get that card so very few times in life," John replied in all seriousness. "It really has a short shelf life." Jessica decided she had had enough of this and started back toward him. She stopped inches away from him. John was trembling from the pain and the lack of use of his legs. Jessica sighed and put his arm around her shoulders.

"Is it so hard to ask for help?" she asked softly.

"It is when you walk away because you're scared," John replied, suddenly very tired.

"I'm not scared," Jessica replied matter-of-factly.

"Yes, you are," John responded. "You're out of excuses of why we can't work. We both are. This thing either works, or it doesn't work because we messed it up. My dead wife, your dead friend, she's out of the picture now; it's just me and you. That's it." Irritated, Jessica looked at him.

"I guess I did ask for you to make the choice," she replied.

"You did, and if you didn't notice, I did make a choice," John replied. Jessica scowled at him.

"I heard," she replied softly. John knew he shouldn't but couldn't help himself. He got one of his famous grins on his face. He knew it was irritating her.

"I'll drop you," she said.

"No, you won't," John replied softly. "You're not dropping me, and I'm not dropping you." Jessica looked away for a second and then back at John.

"That was absolutely, the cheesiest thing I have heard in my entire life," she replied, shaking her head.

"I've been shot," John replied. "I'm not on top of my game."

"I've heard the top of your game, and it's not much better," Jessica retorted, smiling where he couldn't see her. Jessica helped John back to his bed. John lay there with his eyes closed, exhausted. A few minutes later, Lindsey returned to watch him, but Jessica waved her off. Lindsey nodded and left. Jessica sat in the chair and watched him sleep. She never thought she would be in this situation. She knew she loved John, but now that she was finally the love of his life, she realized how scary a real relationship was, especially one involving John Fowler.

"You're staring," John said, never looking at her.

"Sorry," she replied. "I'm just thinking about how you should be careful about what you ask for."

"I'm not quite sure how to take that," John admitted, eyes still closed.

"It was in reference to how I wanted you in my life, and how I wanted you to choose me," Jessica replied.

"Oh," John replied. "So, I'm in your life?"

"Yes, John," Jessica replied, smiling at him. "I can't return you, can I?" John was quiet for a few seconds.

"Jess, I love you," John replied quietly. "But, if you're not comfortable with this relationship, I understand."

"For crying out loud, John," Jessica said. "I'm not dumping you. I was just trying for some fun barbing, but you had to go get all serious on me."

"I'm sorry, Jess. I don't have the energy to barb with you right now," John replied. "How about tomorrow morning?"

"Ok," Jessica replied. "Get some sleep. I'll be here."

"I know," John replied as he drifted off to sleep.

Miami, Florida, Birth Center
Now

Chapter 19

Dr. Nichols had finished giving his statement to the police. He was getting ready to ask if he could leave when he noticed a young man standing by the doorway. Brian tilted his head quickly to the left. The young man nodded and disappeared. Dr. Nichols walked to his office, picked up the completed death certificate, and went to the rear entrance. He made sure no one was looking and stepped outside. The young man from the front was there waiting for Dr. Nichols.

"What happened?" the young man asked.

"The baby was kidnapped," Brian said. The young man, shock covering his face, looked at the death certificate and then back to the doctor. Brian nodded solemnly.

"The men who kidnapped the baby threatened me if I told the police what happened, but Catherine showed up right after the incident occurred, and the police had already been called because of the silent alarm." Brian was shaking as he spoke. The young man shook his head.

"You're scared," he said to Brian simply. The doctor nodded.

"I think we can take care of this, but we need that paperwork filed as quickly as possible," Brian responded. The young man nodded and disappeared into the night. The doctor walked around the building and saw the officer that had taken his statement getting into his car.

The officer began to enter his report electronically. Dr. Nichols had no idea that in Virginia, a program had been created looking for specific things in police reports, and this report was going to set off an alert. Dr. Nichols had no idea that his life was about to change forever.

Moore Home, Virginia
Now

Chapter 20

Chet's phone began to buzz and vibrate. Chet had been asleep for several hours, and he was a little confused when he woke up. After rubbing the sleep from his eyes, he checked his phone and leapt from his bed. He grabbed his laptop and began to download a file. He double checked it and hurried down the hall. He headed downstairs and went into John's room. He paused when he saw Jessica asleep in the chair where the nurse usually sat.

"Boss," Chet whispered. Neither one moved. "Boss!" he said louder.

"Do you think if we continue to ignore him he'll go away?" Jessica asked.

"No," John responded. "It's your turn to feed him. I had him last time." Jessica sat up and looked at John like he was slightly crazy.

"Where did that come from?" Jessica asked.

"I was trying to be funny, but obviously, I'm not. You've shown me the error of my ways," John replied. Jessica gave him a withering look and turned to Chet.

"What's so important that you had to tell us at . . . what time is it?" Jessica asked.

"2:30 in the morning," Chet replied. "I got a hit off the program John told me to run." John sat up in bed and shot Chet a look. Jessica turned toward John, and John gave the most innocent look he could. As Jessica turned back to Chet, John put his finger to his lips. Chet was thoroughly confused.

"Just tell me what Captain Dodo did, Chet," Jessica said. "It's early, or late, or something, and I'm in no mood for his games."

"That hurts," John said, trying to look pitiful. Jessica ignored him.

"John told me to search for any baby kidnappings that were reported by Doctor Nichols," Chet said. Jessica slowly turned to look at John. John was looking all around the room, desperately trying to avoid her gaze.

"And, when did he do that?" Jessica asked, still looking at John while talking to Chet. John had never felt more uncomfortable, and that was saying something, considering he had been shot.

"Right before surgery," Chet said in a very quiet voice. Jessica turned away from John to look at Chet. The look of disbelief on her face was indescribable. John was beginning to think about making a run for it. Of course, he could barely walk at this point, but he had heard of superhuman feats of strength being performed with adrenaline when a human was in the fight or flight scenario. Right now was definite flight!

"He. Did. What?" Jessica asked, pausing after each word. Chet gulped loudly.

Chapter 21

"He asked me right before surgery to set up a program to find out any time anyone in the Nichols family was involved with babies, or kidnappings, or especially baby kidnappings on police reports," Chet responded, shaking from fear. Jessica turned toward John. She spoke to Chet as she glared at John.

"You mean," she began, very quietly but intensely. "When we weren't sure if he was going to survive, and we were only allowed a couple of words with him before surgery, he took the time to ask you to run a check on the Nicholses? Is that what you're saying, Chet?" Chet nodded, but Jessica was staring daggers right into John and didn't notice him. "I can't hear your head rattle, Chet!!"

"Yes!" he replied and fled the room. John envied Chet right then. John thought about running, but he pictured a tiger pouncing a wounded animal when he looked at Jessica. There was no doubt in his mind he was the wounded animal in that scenario, and Jessica was the tiger.

"He ran, didn't he?" she asked. John nodded. "Why would you have Chet do that? What would ever make you think of that, much less when you might be dying!?!"

"I saw Sam," John replied. Jessica nodded. The look on her face told John that she still thought he might have brain damage from the lack of oxygen when he was shot. That, or he was just stupid. John continued. "Sam said the baby was the key. I didn't know what that meant, but something told me I needed to find out more about the Nicholses. Brian Nichols did deliver Sam's baby. It was just a thought, probably brought on by the trauma." John paused. He wasn't completely sure how much to tell Jessica. Part of John believed that the former president, Kenneth Nichols, was involved with Duck and Archibald and whatever their evil scheme was. He was just about positive that Kenneth Nichols was the father of Sam's baby; he had no proof, just a gut feeling. The fact that Kenneth's father was the doctor that delivered Sam's baby bothered John more than he cared to admit. Jessica was walking around the room muttering to herself. She finally spun and began to unload on John.

"You know, I've had a lot going on in my life in the past few weeks. You almost died, I had to tell your parents that you're dead, my lease is almost up, I've been put in charge of a taskforce that only has two members, me and Chet, to bring down one of the most evil men in the world, and the kicker is, on your deathbed, you're following up on leads!" Jessica was close to an emotional breakdown. John missed all of the signs.

"Your lease is almost up?" he asked. "You're not moving, are you?" There was concern on John's face. Jessica stared at him, bug-eyed, and she gave the only reaction she knew to.

"AARGGGHHH!!!" she screamed as she walked out of the room. John sat there for a second trying to figure out what he did. A few seconds later, he saw a head peek around the corner. It was Chet; he had a mini DVD player in his hand and a DVD. He handed John the disc.

"Your funeral," Chet said simply. John beamed. Chet opened the mini-DVD player, and the two watched the funeral before John eventually drifted off to sleep. In the living room, after Jessica had beat a pillow against her head for several minutes, she also drifted off to sleep. Chet headed back to his room with the disc and mini player where he quickly dozed off. After a few minutes, Jessica jerked awake and went back to John's room where she took her spot in the chair in the corner. As she drifted off to sleep, she swore to herself she was going to give John a piece of her mind just as soon as he woke up.

David George
Outside Archibald Staples's Home

Chapter 22

David lay very quiet in the nest he had created. He waited for Archibald to come out to pick up the morning paper. When the door opened and Archibald came out to retrieve it, David trained the sniper rifle on him. David watched Archibald through the scope. All David could figure is that Archibald had watched that mob show and decided he wanted to pick up his own paper. That was the only thing he could think of since the house sat over a half mile from the road, and one of his thugs had to bring the paper up to the front porch every morning.

David smiled as he imagined pulling the trigger, but he knew that would give him no rest. No, the true target was Archibald's daughter Veronica, the former First Lady of the United States of America. Veronica had David's sister, Beth, killed when he was a little boy. Beth had shared her greatest secret with Veronica. Beth was gay, and Veronica, who even at a young age was trying to make an image for herself, became enraged when Beth told her. Veronica was scared that others would think that she was gay since she and Beth had seemed to become best friends.

David snapped out of his thoughts when Archibald suddenly straightened and looked directly where he was buried in his sniper's nest. David smiled to himself. There was no way Archibald saw him. Sure enough, after a couple of minutes, Archibald turned and went inside. David waited for quite some time before he slowly withdrew from his position.

David made the hike back to where his ATV was parked and rode it deep into the forest where his makeshift camp was set up. It would just be a few days now. Since

John Fowler was dead, there was no one else to bring Veronica to justice. David would, and then, he could rest. He could finally rest.

Ronald McGuire
Miami, Florida, Birth Center

Chapter 23

Ronald was trying to take it all in, but it was too much. He had just gotten his orders and couldn't believe them. The Special Agent in Charge, or SAC, had just sent Ronald to learn everything he could about the kidnapping at the birthing center. Apparently, this order came from the top, and as usual, the SAC thought Ronald had something to do with it. Ronald and the SAC had had several blowups in Ronald's first few weeks in North Miami. As he left, the SAC had told Ronald, "Try to play nice. Maybe they'll feel sorry for you and take you home with them."

Ronald knew he didn't fit in at the Miami office. He desperately wanted to work in the New York office, but there had been no open assignments in New York when he graduated. Now with the passing of John Fowler . . . Ronald's thoughts trailed off. He had hoped to work with John, but with his death, that was impossible.

Ronald took a deep breath and surveyed the situation. Ronald knew that two members of John's old team were on their way to Miami. He had been in touch with Director Smothers for months. Director Smothers had wanted someone with Ronald's military background, and Ronald had wanted to be in New York. This was his test. If he passed, then he got what he wanted.

Ronald had been tested his entire life. It started early when he was born to a Caucasian mother and an African-American father. The next test was when his father, a Detroit policeman, was killed. After that was his mother remarrying a Caucasian man that Ronald had come to call his Dad and took his last name. All of those struggles led up to what Ronald thought would be the greatest test of his life, joining Delta Force. Ronald thought that was the end of his trials. He thought he had passed everything there was to pass. That's when life played its cruelest trick on him and had led him to this moment. Ronald had to get to New York. He had hoped when he got there he could work with John Fowler, but that wasn't possible now. Ronald gathered himself and started into the clinic to question the staff and the local police. There was a mystery to solve here. When that was done and Ronald had passed the newest test, it would be time to solve the mystery that currently drove him.

Moore Home
Virginia

Chapter 24

Jessica woke up several hours later but didn't open her eyes. She knew if she opened her eyes and saw John, she was going to have to yell at him, and it was much too early in the morning to be yelling. She was pretty sure it was morning, but she also knew she was being watched. She sighed and decided to play nice.

"Baby, it's very hard to sleep when you just stare at me," she said, still not opening her eyes.

"I apologize," the voice, which clearly wasn't John's, responded. She jerked her eyes open quickly and saw Trip standing in the doorway with a bemused look on his face. "I came with an assignment, but I have to ask you refrain from calling me pet names."

"Trip," Jessica began, but Trip waved her off. Jessica looked around, noticed John wasn't in the room, and looked a little panicked.

"Relax," Trip assured her. "He made his way to the table for breakfast. He looks like he's run a marathon, but he's ok. Does he always complain that much when he tries to walk?" Jessica nodded and ran her hands through her hair, trying to make it look somewhat kept. She noticed Trip looked a little irritated. Trip noticed her noticing and chuckled.

"He did it again," Trip said simply.

"Who?" she asked.

"John," he said and turned and headed out of the room. Jessica hurried after him. When she caught up, Trip continued. "He's right about Dr. Nichols. At least there's something odd there." Irritation washed over Jessica. Trip chuckled. "Only John Fowler can be shot and nearly killed, and manage to work a case at the same time."

"I'm going to kill him," Jessica said quietly. Trip roared with laughter as they entered the dining room. John was sitting with Chet, Arthur, and Henry. Rosa was fussing over John. Chet was having a hard time not laughing over the sight. Jessica came up to Rosa and whispered something in her ear. She hugged Jessica and went into the kitchen. Jessica sat down beside John. Trip took a seat beside Chet, and everyone ate in silence for a minute or so.

"Still planning on killing me?" John asked, never looking at Jessica while reaching for another piece of bacon.

"Maybe," she responded while smacking his hand. John yanked his hand back, shaking it. He shot her a look. "You don't need too much of that. You were just shot. Who knows what the cholesterol in that might do to your arteries?" John looked hurt.

"If I can't have bacon, then maybe someone should just shoot me again," he complained.

"I can fix that for you," she said flatly, while staring daggers at him.

"Enough you two," Trip admonished. "We have a case to work on, not another episode of John and Jessica, The Early Years!"

Chapter 25

"That's got a certain ring to it," John said to Jessica. She glared at him, and John decided he had gone too far again. He turned toward Trip. "I'm sorry. What did you want to talk about?" Trip nodded to Chet.

"Looks like you were right, Boss," Chet said. "Dr. Brian Nichols works predominately with high-risk patients and pregnancies."

"That's what they said about Sam when she was pregnant," Madeline said. "She was considered high-risk, and that's why we stuck with Dr. Nichols." Chet nodded.

"His death rate for babies that are in a high-risk pregnancy are about the lowest in the United States. In fact, if you take his high-risk pregnancies only, the numbers are unbelievably low." Chet paused and looked around the room, not sure how to proceed.

"Go ahead, Chet," John said to him, while working on a piece of toast. "I think I already have a good idea of what you're going to say anyway." Chet nodded.

"Ok," Chet took a deep breath and barreled ahead. "His numbers for normal pregnancy deaths are at the top of the acceptable range." John nodded. It was exactly as he suspected. Trip looked, well, mad, for a lack of a better word. Jessica, Arthur, and Madeline were all a little confused.

"I don't get it," Jessica began. "Maybe I'm sleep deprived, but I just don't get it."

"Why is someone who is the best at what he does with high-risk pregnancies, not one of the best with regular pregnancies?" John asked. The look on Jessica's face said clearly she didn't like what this was implying.

"There's more," Chet said quietly. Jessica shook her head.

"There's always more," Jessica said despondently.

"Most of the mothers of these regular risk pregnancies who have babies that die are single, have little

59

or no family, and are low-income." Chet looked sick as he read the report. "I've read a few case files and was able to get my hands on a few records that have been made public for whatever reason. The doctor has in his notes that he suspects drug use by the mother that led to stillbirth death, or death within seconds of being delivered."

Everyone at the table was very quiet. John looked over at the Moores. They seemed beside themselves. Chet continued.

"The past ten or so years, the doctor has worked specifically with the mothers I have described earlier to try and lower infant stillbirth and death before 28 days of life," Chet finished and looked down at the floor.

"So he has plausible deniability," John said. Trip looked at John sharply.

"He targets mothers who are going to have a hard time raising their children, might have a question of drugs or some type of substance abuse, and might not question their child surviving labor too much," John said, throwing his napkin on the table.

"Why would he do that, John?" Trip asked.

"Who knows why these people do what they do, but it's obvious he's doing something," John responded.

"That's quite a jump, John. We don't know that he's targeting anyone," Trip said. John gave Trip an incredulous look. Trip held up his hand before John could start one of his tirades.

"All we know is some facts don't add up, and now, a child has been kidnapped," Trip said, staring straight at John. John waited, and Trip nodded. "And, it might warrant some investigation." John nodded in approval. "There's a brand new agent down in Miami, Ronald McGuire, that is working the case." Trip turned toward Jessica. "I want you to take point. Ronald is expecting you and Chet." Trip paused. "I want to make it very clear. Our first priority here is finding this kidnapped child and returning it to its parents. Are we clear?" The two agents nodded. "We'll work on Archibald when you two get back." Trip looked at John to make sure there was no objection. John shook his head, surprised.

"A live kidnapped baby is much more important than a dead, irritating FBI agent," John said with a smile on his face. Jessica and Chet had already stood up to get ready to go. Jessica paused and bent down to John's ear.

"You and I are not done talking yet," she said where no one else could hear. She turned and left the room. John looked at Trip seriously.

"Any chance I could get into witness protection and change my name?" John asked as he reached for more bacon. Trip reached over, smacked John's hand, making John yank it back. Trip picked up the bacon, and began to eat it while shaking his head no.

"You, too?" John asked. "You're mad at me, too?" Trip just stared at John and nodded as he ate the bacon. John sighed and began what he felt was a three thousand mile walk back to his room.

Chapter 26

Chet met John before he reached his room. John gladly took the break.

"We need to talk," Chet said quietly. John looked around, saw they were alone, and nodded at Chet to go ahead. "Look, it's none of my business, but I think Jessica is more than a little freaked out." John looked at his friend, confused. "John, she heard you that day about choosing her over Sam." John nodded, still confused. Chet was a little frustrated. He knew his friend could be dense when it came to the opposite sex. "Dude, you gave up being reunited with Sam, and you tracked down her killer. It was one of those perfect romantic endings that women love!" John looked at his friend like he had lost his mind.

"Yeah, there's nothing better than solving someone's murder and dying to be with them. Heaven knows being dead is what we're all striving for each day," John responded.

"What about Romeo and Juliet?" Chet asked.

"They were still dead," John replied. "I get it. Okay, so I really don't, but I understand what you're trying to say. The best I can give you is we're out of excuses. She can't say I picked Sam over her any longer." Chet sighed and nodded.

"She told me on the car ride down here that the whole you coming back from the dead thing was kind of hard to deal with," Chet tried to explain. "It's like you made the ultimate sacrifice."

"Uh, no," John replied. "The ultimate sacrifice would be if I took a bullet for her, which I would."

"You may have to take one for Chet," Jessica said from around the corner where she had been standing, listening to the conversation. The color drained from Chet's face, and he fled. Jessica walked around the corner to John. She stopped just in front of him.

"Don't be mad at him," John began. "You knew he was going to tell me."

"Yeah, I did," Jessica replied, a playful smile forming on her mouth. "So, about this dead thing." She stopped and looked at John, not sure what to say.

"What about trying to take it one day at a time?" John offered. Jessica took John's hands and nodded. "That's not what's bothering you, is it?" Jessica shook her head no. "I'm going to take a shot that it might have something to do with me telling you I love you, and you telling me you love me." Jessica nodded slowly. John pressed on. "So, you think because it was a traumatic time that we admitted we love each other that what we have is doomed to fail?" Jessica nodded. "Is this a traumatic time?" Jessica shook her head no. "I love you," John said simply. Jessica stood there. John looked down the hallway and didn't see anyone. He shouted. "Trip, Chet, Madeline, Arthur, I love Jessica!" Jessica started to laugh in spite of herself. Heads started to slowly pop into the hallway, like prairie dogs.

"And, I love him," she shouted. Jessica turned back to him, smiling. "And, I promise you I'm going to kill him if he ever pulls a stunt like that again."

"We know," the others chorused together. Jessica kissed John and helped him back to his room. After she was satisfied she was ready to go, she prepared to leave for the new case. She promised to call him when they landed in Miami. As she left, John reminded her that he was dead, so she'd have to be careful calling him. Jessica, Chet and Trip left the Moores', leaving John to his thoughts. After a minute or so, John called Rosa to his room to see about getting him a few things. He had a thought where his friends might end up when this had all played out, and if he was right, he wanted to be in a position to help them.

Chapter 27

John flipped on the TV while waiting for Rosa to bring him what he asked for. He flipped over to one of the numerous news channels that claimed to be the only one that was fair and impartial. John didn't watch the news often, mostly because he tended to know more about a situation than was being reported. Today was a different day. He was afraid he might be late, but he had turned the TV on just in time to see his friend, Jeremiah Cosby, put his hand on a Bible. Jeremiah spoke, and John listened, his heart bursting with pride.

"I do solemnly swear that I will support and defend the Constitution of the United States against all enemies, foreign and domestic; that I will bear true faith and allegiance to the same; that I take this obligation freely, without any mental reservation or purpose of evasion; and that I will well and faithfully discharge the duties of the office on which I am about to enter: So help me God."

John nodded in appreciation at his friend, the new Vice President of the United States. John reached up and rubbed his chest gently where the bullet had gone through him. While he was happy for his friend, he had two more monsters, and possibly a third, to hunt down. Archibald Staples and Kenneth Nichols were number one and two on his list to bring down. John knew he had nothing on Kenneth but a gut feeling, but John trusted his gut. There was something not right about the former president. What bothered him more than anything was he sat across from him not very long ago and didn't pick anything up from him. There were a couple of possible reasons. One was that Kenneth was the President of the United States, and John wasn't looking for anything or ignored anything he might have felt because of who he was. John had played back the conversation he, Trip, and the president had that day. John could find nothing that indicated the president had lied to him. To be honest, the conversation had been steered by Kenneth in a way that he was never forced to lie. That was a very plausible explanation. Of course, there was another explanation, one that chilled John to his core. He could be like Bruce. Kenneth could be a sociopath, and that was why John couldn't get a read on him. John had brought down Bruce. He knew, eventually, he would bring down Archibald, but how was he going to bring down one of the most popular presidents of the United States?

Kenneth Nichols
Washington, D.C.

Chapter 28

Kenneth sat in his home, watching the television. He was watching Jeremiah being sworn into the Vice-Presidency. The thought sickened his stomach.

"Why do you keep watching that, Dad? You know all it does is make you mad," the young woman called from the kitchen.

"I'm remembering this low moment of my life, so when I'm back on top, I'll remember how far I've come," he replied. "Are you sure you want to go through with this?"

"It's time for me to be the person I was born to be," she replied. Kenneth smiled.

"I'm proud of you, and I'm sure your mother would have been too," he said simply.

"Good-bye," she said as the back door shut behind her. With that, she was gone. Kenneth didn't know when he would see her again. He laughed to himself. In all the years he had been married to his wife, she had never known about his daughter. The fact that Veronica's own father knew and she didn't had amused him.

Kenneth got up from his chair and headed into his study. He logged into his bank account from an overseas holding company. The amount of money in the account was staggering. Was it time for him to simply retire to some island somewhere? Should he call his daughter and tell her that her plan wasn't necessary? Kenneth laughed out loud at the thought. That was the thing that his ex-wife had never understood. When you lost, you didn't get even; you got ahead. Heads were going to roll over what happened to him; it was just a matter of time.

Kenneth picked up the remote on his desk and turned the television back on to watch more of the coverage of the inauguration. The ticker running across the bottom of the screen caught his eye. It mentioned a baby kidnapping in Miami. Kenneth groaned. His father was in Miami. He did a quick online search, and sure enough, the center his father ran was in the middle of what had happened. His father knew the consequences. He opened a drawer in his desk and pulled out the red burner cellphone he kept for emergencies. He called his friend in Florida to tell him what he had learned. His friend in Florida assured Kenneth that now that he was aware of the situation, he would keep an eye on it and tell Kenneth anything he learned. Kenneth was sure his father would have to be dealt with. After all, he would demand the same out of his friend if his father had made such an error.

Jessica Hammerstein
On an Airplane to Miami

Chapter 29

Jessica stared out the window at the ground below. She had no idea how high up she was in the air. She was nervous for the first time in a long time. What surprised her most was what she was nervous about. She was back in charge of the unit. She had been from the time John left the FBI until he came back. It didn't bother her that her last time as team leader had led to failure. Sam's case had been nearly impossible to solve, and in the end, only John had been able to put all of the pieces together. While she was happy spending the rest of her FBI career with Chet and John, she knew if she failed this time, there would never be the opportunity for her to get her own team.

Jessica sighed and looked out the window again. It was bad enough that her brother and one of her sisters was a lawyer, another sister was a doctor, and her last sister was an accountant. They were all successful and very well-off financially. Her parents thought she wasn't grounded because she had wanted to be a dancer. Jessica really wanted to scream. What drove her even crazier was the fact she had just found out before John got shot that he was loaded. Filthy, stinking rich, and he didn't care. Of course it is easy not to care when you don't have to worry about paying for the refrigerator when it starts making those funny noises. She was still a little peeved that Arthur had her student loans forgiven a few weeks ago, but she had to admit it had freed up her finances some.

What bothered Jessica the most, if she would admit it, was she had gone away to prove to the world that she could be something, and now that she was, she found out it really didn't change anything. She was happy with who she was, and she found out she didn't care what people thought of her. It really was time to patch things up with her parents. One thing John's shooting had taught her was that no one ever knew how much time they had in this life.

She felt content for just a second, and then, the thoughts of her lease crept back in her head. She pushed the thoughts out of her mind. She looked over at Chet who was stuck with some chatty Kathy that had the seat between them. Chet had blamed himself so much for John being shot. Even after the doctors told them that John would most likely survive, Chet was upset with himself for days. The two men had a special bond that Jessica envied some days.

The plane began to descend, and in a few minutes, the plane coasted to a stop. Jessica turned her cellphone on and found she had a text message. She was somewhat nervous about opening it. John was very deficient when it came to phones, tablets, and VCRs for that matter. The other day, she had noticed he had a piece of duct tape over the area where the clock was supposed to be on his VCR. Why he still had one, she wasn't for sure. She finally pealed it back to see if what she suspected was true. Sure enough, the time was flashing 12:00. She asked him if he knew how to program the clock, and he danced all around the subject. She decided to let it go, but she knew the answer.

She looked at the text. "Jess, it's John. I know you're worried about this case, but you'll do fine. I love you. Is that okay to type? Will someone see this that shouldn't? If you're reading this and shouldn't be, it's not really John. He's dead."

Jessica didn't know whether to laugh, cry, or sign John up for a class to learn how to text.

Chapter 30

Jessica and Chet arrived at the crime scene at the birthing center. She informed the local authorities who she was and told them she was not here to steal their case, but only help.

"Lady," the senior detective on the scene replied. "You can have this case. It's going to be a nightmare. I'll do everything I can to help you close it, but I have too many open cases on me to want to be responsible for something like this."

Jessica nodded and headed inside the clinic. She had noticed when dealing with local police, there were usually two initial reactions. The first was for the local authorities to fight for their case. Jessica respected that approach; the case meant something to them, and they wanted to solve it. The second, what she had just witnessed, bothered her. She was sure the detective would do all he could, but he had become so caught up in the bureaucracy, or his superior had, that the life had been sucked out of him. She looked around for the local FBI agent that was supposed to help Chet and her on this case.

She spotted a man that stood out from the rest of the authorities on the scene. Jessica quickly sized him up. He appeared to be of African-American descent and was tall, lean, and fit. He carried himself with a certain confidence. Jessica knew he had to have military training. She stopped for a second. How had she known that? Was this the result of her pestering John to teach her how to read people? In the past few weeks when they went out, one of things Jessica had John do was just look at random people as they sat at a cafe or coffee shop and tell her why he thought what he thought about people.

Jessica took another look at the man and looked around for Chet. She found him and walked over to him.

"Chet," she whispered. "Does our contact have military training?" Chet gave her a look but pulled out the file he had on Ronald and scanned it. He nodded and then raised his head, his brow furrowed in a question.

"How did you know that?" he asked. Jessica just smiled. Jessica walked over to the man she saw earlier. As soon as he noticed her, Jessica extended her hand.

"Ronald McGuire, I am Jessica Hammerstein. Welcome to the team," she stated with confidence. Ronald smiled in surprise and shook her hand.

"Ron, if you'd please. I'm glad to be here," he replied. "Picture in my file?" he asked. Jessica shook her head.

"I don't know. I haven't seen it," she replied and led him into a room where no one else was around. Ron looked slightly surprised. Jessica now understood why John enjoyed this so. She waved in Chet to join them. When all three were in the room, she shut the door.

"Ok, Ron," she began. "You might as well bring us up to speed."

Chapter 31

Ron checked his notes and began.

"According to the reports gathered from the multiple eyewitnesses, it seems that around 2 A.M. somewhere between 5 and 40 men dressed with presidential masks entered the clinic armed with anything between small handguns to bazookas." Ron looked up from his notes at his two new colleagues. Jessica and Chet couldn't help but smile.

"Gotta love eyewitness testimony," Chet replied. Jessica could only nod. "Any chance of there being any surveillance cameras?" Ron nodded.

"Yep," Ron replied. "We have seven figures we can count on the tape near the entrance, but it was a bad angle. There could have been more that entered the clinic. I can tell you there was no bazooka on the seven I saw." Ron looked back down at his notes and continued.

"What the eyewitnesses do agree on is there was a baby stolen. Carrie Williams had given birth earlier that night, and she was resting in her room with her husband Mark when the gang broke in and stole the child." Ron looked up from his notes at Chet and Jessica. A grim look was on all of their faces.

"What about the nurse that was watching the child in the nursery?" Jessica asked. Ron shook his head.

"No nurse," he replied. "According to the doctor, they had all been working double shifts because of the amount of babies that had been delivered in the past few days. He knew Catherine was supposed to be coming in at 3 A.M. Apparently, this was a lull, so he had sent everyone home, and Catherine was only going to be here in case an emergency arose. Apparently, the Williamses came in sometime around midnight. Brian Nichols did not call anyone in and delivered the baby by himself. According to Dr. Nichols, the mother seems to be just fine physically. The doctor admits he should have had more staff here in case something went wrong, but he insists there was nothing negligent on his part."

"Perfect storm," Chet said quietly. Jessica turned to look at him. "Think about it. Only one doctor and the family to subdue to get the baby."

"You think the doctor was in on it?" Ron asked. "While I admit things look a little suspicious, the doctor was visibly shaken when I talked to him. I'm not saying he wasn't involved, but if he is, he just fooled me."

Jessica smiled. "Maybe I should question him."

"He's been released along with the Williamses," Ron said. Jessica stared at him. "They had all been through an ordeal. The doctor has been working way too many hours, and Mrs. Williams had just given birth. Everyone was starting to get upset, so a compromise was made. Officers went with the Williamses and the doctor under the guise of being there in case someone called with a ransom demand."

Jessica didn't look thrilled, but she nodded in acceptance.

"Whose idea was it to send the officers home with the witnesses?" she asked. Ron looked a little uncomfortable.

"That was all my idea," Ron admitted. "Catherine is still here if you want to interview her."

"That's good work, Agent," Jessica admitted. With that, she turned and left the room. Ron walked over toward Chet.

"That's the agent they call The Hammer, isn't it?" Ron asked. Chet nodded. "She doesn't look like what I would have imagined." Chet chuckled.

"That's what makes it so much fun to watch when she interviews them," he said heading out the door, leaving Ron to catch up.

Chapter 32

Jessica had a police report and a copy of the detective's notes. She was walking the crime scene, not that there was much to see. She noticed Chet and Ron talking, seemingly more excited by the moment. If Jessica didn't know better, she would think that Ron seemed somewhat in awe of Chet. She wondered if Ron was a closet computer gamer. Chet did have a certain reputation around the bureau. Truth be told, the whole team all had a certain reputation around the bureau. Jessica shook the thoughts from her mind. They had to find this child and fast. To Jessica, it didn't seem like this was a kidnapping/ransom case. This seemed more like an abduction.

As Jessica walked back to the main room, she saw one of the nurses who looked very upset.

"Catherine?" Jessica asked as she walked up to her. Catherine looked at Jessica with confusion. "I'm Agent Hammerstein with the FBI. Can we talk?"

A look of relief spread across Catherine's face. Jessica led her to an empty room. Jessica wanted this to be as informal and casual as possible. If Catherine was comfortable, she was more likely to say something that could help even if she didn't know it was important.

"I just have a few questions," Jessica began. Catherine nodded. Jessica smiled and began. "You arrived after the abduction happened?" Catherine nodded, angry.

"If I've told that man once, I've told him a thousand times. It doesn't matter how tired we are; there needs to be more than just him here for a delivery," Catherine said, very irritated. She leaned in to Jessica, and Jessica leaned in to her. Jessica learned long ago if you mimicked the movements of the other person, it would help gain their trust. Catherine had a lot to say, and Jessica wanted her to say every word of it.

"I know we're not a traditional hospital," she began. "But, there has to be more than just the doctor around in case something goes wrong. I have no problem with just the doctor being in with the delivery, or just one of the midwives, but someone else must be around in case something goes wrong. I know we have all been working ourselves to death the past few days, but we owe it to our patients to be here and to be prepared for them. He promised me this wouldn't happen again. Don't get me wrong. I don't think me being here would have changed the outcome of this kidnapping, but if I was here, who knows?" Catherine sat back, fuming. Jessica was running everything through her mind when Catherine leaned back in.

"You know, I swear he does this to prove he still has it," Catherine said in a low voice as if it were a secret between the two.

"I don't understand," Jessica replied.

"He gets like this after he loses one of those children at the hospital. It's not his fault those parents don't tell him the truth up front. He's one of the best in the world, but he can only save those kids if he has all of the facts." Catherine had a frown on her face.

"Did he lose a child at the hospital?" Jessica asked, trying to keep herself calm while thinking about the conversation that had taken place back in Virginia.

"There was a still-birth at the hospital three days ago," Catherine said like it should be common knowledge. Suddenly, she got a guilty look on her face. "He hasn't filed the paperwork yet, has he?"

"What do you mean?" Jessica asked.

"The death certificate he was supposed to file. He was probably late, given how busy he's been," Catherine said with a worried look. Jessica smiled and laid a reassuring hand on Catherine's arm.

75

"I'm not worried about some tardy paperwork, Catherine," Jessica replied comfortingly. "I'm trying to reunite a couple with their baby." Jessica made a mental note to come back to this in a less invasive way. "What can you tell me about them, the Williamses I mean?"

"Nothing," Catherine replied. "I never saw them before tonight."

Chapter 33

Jessica was trying to hold in her shock and surprise. Catherine noticed and chuckled. She waved her hand as she talked, as if to say, you misunderstand.

"Oh, that happens all the time," Catherine began. "These clinics aren't well known, and sometimes, it takes the entire pregnancy before the couple is comfortable coming here. Dr. Nichols had been their OB/GYN the entire time, and in the end, they decided to try the clinic."

Jessica nodded. "Anything odd happen this week?" Catherine shook her head no. She looked at Jessica, bit her bottom lip, and then spoke.

"Well, not odd, odd," Catherine began. "Like I said before, it's just what he does sometimes. We were swamped the past few days, so he contacted all his patients and asked them to use the hospital should they get ready to give birth. You have to understand. We are a small staff; that's why I found it odd about the Williamses coming in. On the other hand, he's done this before; deliver a baby with no one else here when he loses a child that wasn't designated high-risk." She paused and sighed. "The mothers are so worried about being judged for their lifestyle that they won't tell us what really is going on in their lives." She shook her head, and tears formed in her eyes. "They don't understand what it does to him; every death affects him personally. He almost gets physically ill when it happens." Jessica gave Catherine a look of sympathy.

"Does he take every death so hard?" Jessica asked.

"No," she replied. "In the cases of high-risk, he is able to prepare for them; it's the ones he thinks would not have happened if he had known."

"You mentioned some paperwork that he was late on. Is this child we're talking about the one that passed away?" Jessica asked. Catherine nodded. Jessica continued. "Is he late often on the paperwork?" The look

77

on Catherine's face was reminiscent of a wife who had been married many years talking about something her husband constantly messes up.

"He tends to be forgetful," Catherine replied. Jessica smiled at her.

"So the death that happened a few days ago, do you know the mother's name?" Jessica asked.

"I think it was Christina Lopez," Catherine replied. "You don't think she had anything to do with this, do you?"

"No, nothing like that," Jessica replied, smiling. "I just need to ask her some questions to eliminate her from the suspect list. I need to make sure I follow up every single lead." Jessica leaned in close and spoke in a low voice. "Some of these guys think whatever they want to do is ok." Catherine nodded and touched Jessica's arm to show she completely understood. Jessica was proud of herself for nailing that one. Part of her wondered if Christina could have stolen the child since she lost her own, especially if she was using drugs the way Catherine and Dr. Nichols implied. Maybe they had all been wrong. Maybe Dr. Nichols was the great doctor he seemed to be, and he was just working in hard conditions, or maybe he was exactly what they thought. Regardless, Jessica was going to follow the evidence and go with it, wherever it led her.

Chapter 34

Jessica walked out of the room with Catherine and noticed a lack of police presence. Lack was the incorrect word. No presence would be the correct words, as in there was no one from the local PD on the scene. Chet saw her and waved her into another room. She walked in, and Chet closed the door behind her. Ron was already in the room.

"It's just the FBI," Chet said. Jessica raised an eyebrow. "Local PD has completely turned the case over to us. They think it was a either a bunch of addicts that stole the baby to sell for drugs, or a crazed girlfriend of one of the gang members put them up to it." Jessica blew air up from her bottom lip.

"The Miami bureau?" Jessica asked while turning toward Ron. "Where are they on this?"

"You have the full resources, but it's going to be the newer agents like me," Ron replied.

"Fine with me," Jessica replied. "You've already shown good work on this case. I'll gladly take agents that want to solve this case, regardless of their rank or experience." Ron smiled broadly at Jessica. "Besides," she continued. "It's not like this is your first job taking orders." Ron looked at her, never blinking. "Where did you serve?"

"I'm sorry, but that's classified," Ron answered simply. Jessica could tell by the tone that Ron didn't want to discuss it as much as he wasn't allowed to discuss it, and she let it go. She moved where she could see both men and began to get on with the case. "I want you to check all medical records you can online. Check Dr. Nichols' bank accounts for anything fishy, and check to see if all the proper paperwork has been filed on the death of Christina Lopez's son. I want you to go to the hospital. Ask around about Christina Lopez. She wouldn't be the first mother to lose a child and then do something crazy." Jessica turned to leave, and so did Ron when Chet waved his hand to stop him. Ron shook his head no, but Chet ignored him.

"Which one of us did you want to go to the hospital?" Chet asked. Jessica stopped with a confused look on her face.

"You're the computer guru, Chet," Jessica responded. Chet shook his head.

"Chet," Ron began, but Chet waved him off.

"Ron is just as good as me," Chet responded. Jessica slightly jerked back in surprise. Chet continued. "He's self-taught, but he can -" Jessica cut him off.

"I'm not as bad as John about computer lingo, but you'll just confuse me, Chet," Jessica replied. "If you vouch for him, it's good enough for me." She paused. "Is there another reason?" Chet nodded.

"Maybe I want to see what else I can do," he replied. Jessica smiled and nodded. She understood exactly what he meant.

"You know what this case means to me?" she asked. Chet nodded. "So you know I understand what you just said." Chet nodded again. "Then I'm fine with what either of you two do, but if there comes a point where he's stumped-" Ron interrupted.

"Trust me, if I'm in over my head, I have no problem with asking him for help," Ron interjected. Chet started to head out the door and clapped Ron on the shoulder as he walked by.

"I'll do it if need be, Jess," Chet replied. "But, I highly doubt it's needed." Ron smiled at the compliment. He pointed back and forth between the two.

"You two are impressive," Ron said. "I've always heard what a great team you are, and it shows. It's impressive you run this well, considering." Jessica froze, and so did Chet. They both realized at the same time that they were supposed to have just lost a teammate. They both turned to face Ron, not sure what to say. Ron misread the looks on their faces and thought he had just stepped in it. "Oh, crap." Jessica shook her head and waved it off.

"When we work," Jessica began, looking at Chet for support. "We're in our element." Chet nodded.

"It's what he would have wanted," Chet continued. "It's a way of honoring his legacy." Ron nodded. Jessica thought she was going to throw up in her mouth with that line that Chet just served.

"I'm sorry," Ron said simply and headed out the door. They watched him go, and Jessica leaned closer to Chet.

"It's a way of honoring his memory?" she asked softly, in disbelief.

"It just popped out," he replied.

"Don't ever say something like that again," she responded. "For one thing, if he ever heard you say that, there would be no stopping his ego. Secondly, you about made me burst out laughing or vomit; I'm not for sure which." Chet nodded and headed out of the room. Jessica shook her head.

Chapter 35

Jessica accompanied Ron back to his office. She waited while he ran the records of Christina Lopez. He began running different searches for hospital records, bank accounts, and other things Jessica asked for.

"Want to come with me to Christina's house?" Jessica offered. Ron shook his head no.

"I'd love to Agent Hammerstein, but some of these clowns here might do something to the searches while they're running," he replied. Jessica looked shocked. She leaned in.

"Is it racial?" she asked. Ron laughed, and Jessica leaned back in surprise.

"No," he replied. "Agent Hammerstein-" Jessica cut him off.

"Jessica," she replied. "Or Jess."

"Jessica," he continued with a smile on his face. "I've dealt with racial problems my whole life. I grew up not accepted by either race." Jessica looked a little confused. "I'm bi-racial," he explained. Jessica nodded. "What's going on here seems to be something totally different," he paused and looked frustrated. "When I got here, I made the mistake of saying how I'd like to work in New York. That statement has been held against me ever since. Between that and my military background, everyone thinks that I think I'm too good for this position. I thought if I worked hard, everyone would come around. Well, I was wrong there. Everyone now thinks I'm just working my tail off to get out of here." Jessica shook her head. Ron bit his bottom lip and then decided to go ahead and go for it. "Any chance of me coming to New York after this is over?" Jessica looked at Ron, not sure how to answer.

"It's not really my call, Ron," she replied. Ron nodded.

"Ok," he replied. He stared at the computer for a minute. "I guess it was in bad taste for me to ask, given what you and Chet have been through." Jessica patted Ron on the shoulder and decided the best way to handle this was to get going on the investigation.

"I need to go interview some people," she said, turned, and left the office. As Ron watched her walk away, he chided himself. He knew he was pushing things too far too fast, but New York was where he needed to get to. He stared at the computer screen for a minute and then opened a drawer in his desk. He pulled out a file and began to look through it. There were numerous pictures of murder victims. There were male and female victims. All the victims were Caucasian. The women were all blond, and the men all had brown hair. He paused at one particular picture for a minute. Ron knew every detail in the folder by heart, but he knew this picture the best. He shook his head, closed the file, and put it back in his desk drawer. He was getting to New York, whether Jessica would help him or not.

Chapter 36

Jessica headed to the address that Ronald had given her. Jessica had to admit to herself she was considering what Ron had asked her. They could use someone like him in the New York office. Jessica really liked what she had seen from Ron so far in the investigation. He was determined, efficient, knew how to get things done, and honestly, he was easy on the eyes. Jessica smiled and wondered how John would react to Ron being in New York. Both of them had that alpha dog personality about them. Jessica pushed John from her head. She needed to work on this case and not worry about John. She did miss him. Jessica had to admit she had enjoyed John being back at the FBI. There was something special when the three of them worked a case.

Jessica pulled up to the address she was given and looked around the apartment building. It seemed to be in pretty good shape. There were some places that gave off the vibe of being a drug den, but this place didn't give that feeling. There were some young men sitting on the step, and Jessica prepared herself for a verbal exchange. She got out of the car and walked over toward them.

"Are you lost, Miss?" the one that seemed to be the leader called out.

"No, I'm here to see someone. I'm FBI," she said as she showed them the badge. The group passed a look between them. They looked nervous. Jessica sized them up. They could have been some of the men in the video that raided the clinic. "I'm not looking for trouble," she said. "I just have to interview someone."

"You won't get any trouble out of us," the leader said. "We're here to keep trouble away." Jessica smiled.

"I hope you're not using weapons," she said.

"Nope," the leader replied. "Christina wouldn't like that." Jessica looked surprised.

"Christina Lopez?" Jessica asked. The leader nodded. "Is she here?"

"No ma'am," the leader responded. "She and her baby left this morning." Jessica's eyebrows went up.

"I thought Christina's child died during childbirth," Jessica replied. The leader of the group got a very steely look on his face.

"No, ma'am, she didn't," he said very determined. "She had to leave her baby in the hospital for a few days, but she brought him home this morning. They left today to stay with her parents for a while since her husband is not around anymore."

"Did her husband leave her?" Jessica asked. A few of the boys looked sad. The leader spoke in a softer voice.

"No, ma'am," he replied. "His name was Oscar; he died overseas in the fighting." Jessica was beyond confused. The only thing that made sense at this point was the poor woman had a mental break and had gotten these young men to help her. This case was beginning to depress her by the second.

"Last question and I'll leave you alone," she said. The leader nodded for her to continue. "Do any of you think she might have been doing drugs?" Each one of the men burst into laughter. Jessica was utterly confused. When the laughter died down the leader spoke.

"You're funny, lady," he began. "Oscar and Christina started our little watch here, to make sure there were no drugs being sold in the neighborhood." Jessica looked at them, letting it all sink in. "Christina has been fighting the drug trade in this city for the past three years!"

Ron and Chet
FBI Headquarters, Miami

Chapter 37

Chet returned to the Miami headquarters and found Ron going through the reports he had run.

"Find anything helpful?" Chet asked when Ron looked up and saw him. Ron shook his head no.

"Nothing that stands out," Ron replied. He pushed back from his desk and looked up at Chet. "I think I blew it with Agent Hammerstein." Chet looked a little confused. "I asked her if it was possible for me to join you two in New York when this is all over."

"That's not her call, Ron," Chet replied. Ron gave Chet a strange look.

"That's exactly what she said," Ron replied. "Is there something going on?" Chet quickly shook his head no.

"Nothing like that," Chet replied. "The New York office is just going to take its time and see what is the best fit for our team. That's all." Ron didn't look like he believed Chet but decided to let it go.

"Did you find out anything at the hospital?" Ron asked, changing the subject.

"Maybe," Chet replied. "The nurse that normally works for Dr. Nichols wasn't there. Apparently, she is the unofficial head of the nursery for any babies he delivers. The nurse I talked to, an Emma Marcia, seemed nervous when I questioned her."

"Think she had something to do with it?" Ron asked. "Emma, I mean."

"No, not exactly," Chet said, thinking. "I think she knows something though. She acted really funny when I questioned her. I think Jessica needs to have a run at Emma."

"What about the nurse in charge of the nursery, unofficially?" Ron asked.

"Something's not right there," Chet responded. "Emma seemed scared of her, like she shouldn't cross her. I have her information right here. Her name is Sheila Long." Chet paused. "I hate to ask, but you did run checks overseas to make sure the doctor didn't have a Swiss account or something like that?" Ron gave Chet a withering look.

"Come on, man," Ron replied. "I'm not some newbie. I went through all the channels. Since we're dealing with a baby kidnapping case, we're allowed to know if anyone we ask about involved in this case has an account but not how much is in there." Chet chuckled.

"Actually, you are a newbie to the FBI," Chet replied, smiling. Ron chuckled and began working on the computer. Chet watched him. "You're going to check out both Sheila and Emma?" Ron nodded.

"I could be wrong, but I'd rather have tried than do nothing," he replied. He turned toward Chet. "You hungry?" Chet nodded. "I think it will be ok if we go out and hit a food truck. I know a place that I think you'll love." Chet thought that sounded like the best idea anyone had all day. As they left the computer and walked out the door, an icon on the computer monitor started flashing. It had found an account under one of the names they had searched for. The screen continued to blink as other agents walked through the office, never noticing what was going on.

Jessica Hammerstein
Miami, Florida

Chapter 38

Jessica was trying to process what she had been told. These young men had told her that not only did Christina not have a drug problem, but that she and her husband had organized a group of citizens to stop the drug dealers in this area. On top of that, according to the men, Christina's baby did not die but was in the hospital for a few days and had been brought home that morning.

This was making her head hurt. What was worse, for a split second, she had wished John was there to see who was lying. She had to admit, having a human lie detector made things much simpler. Jessica cleared all thought of John from her mind. John wasn't here, and she didn't need him to solve this case. She was going to figure this thing out, but it was clear this wasn't as cut and dry as she'd first thought. Either Christina had been lying to these young men for years and had a habit that no one knew about which led to the death of her son, or something else was going on here. The worst part of it was this was not getting her any closer to finding the Williamses' baby.

"Are you ok, Lady?" the leader of the group asked. Jessica pressed her lips together and nodded.

"I am, thank you. What's your name?" Jessica asked.

"Felipe. Felipe Marcia," he told her confidently. Jessica smiled and nodded.

"Felipe, there was a baby kidnapping this morning at the birthing center. A couple had their newborn child kidnapped. Did any of you hear anything about it?" Jessica stared at Felipe, looking for any signs during his answer.

"Let me guess," Felipe said with venom in his voice. "Some rich white couple had their child kidnapped, and the entire world comes running to help. Let a couple of us die here in the streets, and no one bothers to show up until the bodies start smelling."

Something that Felipe said just tickled the back of Jessica's brain.

"Felipe, will you wait here a second? There's something I need to check." She waited until Felipe nodded. He looked very confused. Jessica walked over to the car and started flipping through records. She found exactly what she was looking for. Carrie Williams was born in the United States, but both her mother and father had originally been born in Cuba. She didn't want to jump to any conclusions, so she closed the file and walked back over to Felipe.

"Thank you," she said to him. Felipe nodded. "Felipe, a baby was kidnapped. I am working under the belief that the baby is alive. I have no idea how things normally work around here, and for that, I apologize. But I promise you I would work this kidnapping case as hard as possible, regardless of the baby's race, ethnicity, gender, or any other trait. Do you understand?" Felipe nodded. He didn't like it, but he understood.

"I haven't heard anything about any rich white baby being kidnapped," he replied quietly. Jessica smiled and handed him her card.

"If you hear anything, about any baby, will you please let me know?" she asked. Felipe never answered but took her card. She nodded and headed back to her car with a thought in the back of her brain that wouldn't go away.

Chapter 39

As Jessica drove back to the Miami FBI office, she began to make a mental checklist of everything she needed to do. She needed to interview the Williamses, she needed to interview Dr. Nichols, she needed to interview anyone that Chet found at the hospital that may know anything, and she needed to do a complete background check on Christina and Oscar Lopez. Anyone who had started a group like they had would have had press coverage, whether they wanted it or not. Not only that, but if she could find a photograph of them and any of the young men she had seen today, then maybe Chet and Ron could use their computer skills to match up the picture to the video at the birth center.

As she thought of all these things, her mind drifted to John. What would John do that she hadn't thought of? It wasn't that she didn't trust her abilities because she did. But, when you have one of the best at your side, if you don't pick up on some of his good habits, then you've wasted an opportunity.

She had searched the crime scene from top to bottom. She had a list of suspects to talk to. She had made some progress, strange progress, but progress all the same. She was following up on those leads. What was she missing that John would have done? She looked at the phone and decided to call him. She picked it up and dialed the number. After a few rings, the familiar voice answered on the other end.

"Hello," John said.

"John, it's Jess," she replied. "I need to tell you about this case and see what I've missed."

"Ok," John replied. He sat and listened as Jessica told him the entire case. She actually arrived at her destination while she was talking. She stayed in the car and kept talking. She told him of her list of people to interview, leads she was following, and what her plans were. When she finished, she waited to hear what John had to say.

"Sounds good," John said. Jessica was flabbergasted. She was silent for a second. "Jess, are you still there?" he asked.

"I'm here," she responded. "Is there something else you would have done?"

"Well," he began. Here it is, she thought. "I probably would have eaten lunch at some point." Jessica stared at the phone for a few seconds, shocked. She was sure she had missed something. "Jess?" he asked at her silence.

"I'm still here," she answered. "Are you sure I haven't missed anything? You know the last case I ran, I almost got me and Chet fired."

"Jess, knock it off," John said. Jessica was stunned. "If I was doing this, what would you say to me?"

"Put your big boy pants on and quit crying?" Jessica asked more than stated.

"Exactly," John responded. "You're one of the best, so act like it."

"Yes, sir!" she replied, smiling.

"Hey, Jess," John said quietly. "Just don't get so good that you don't need me every once in a while."

"I'll try, John," she replied. "John, thank you. Love you."

"I love you," John replied, a little surprised. "Is everything all right?"

"It is now," she said. "I've got to go. I'll call you later."

"Ok, bye," John said and disconnected. Jessica sat in the car with a smile on her face. She was going to solve this case. Then, she would solve her love life.

Bruce Cosby
Secret Medical Facility

Chapter 40

Bruce opened his eyes. Everything was blurry, and he felt very groggy. His chest was hurting. He went to rub it when his arm was rudely stopped from moving. He sat up as much as he could and looked down at the cuff that was on his wrist attached to the bed. He glanced over to the other hand and saw it was cuffed to the bed as well. Bruce had forgotten about being restrained. With all the pain medicine pumping through him, he wasn't surprised. Bruce lay back in the bed and tried to get comfortable. He knew he needed to exercise his mind to work through the fog, so he thought about the incident that had landed him in this current predicament. Four bullets had ripped through him, and it hadn't been enough to stop him. Bruce chuckled to himself. He took out John Fowler with one bullet, and four bullets couldn't stop him.

Bruce began to try to think about what had happened in the past few days. He tried to push the drug-induced haze from his mind. His lawyer had seen him; when, he wasn't completely sure. Bruce began to chuckle until he almost sounded insane. One of the armed guards outside his door heard him and looked in the window, bothered. That made Bruce laugh even more. He was going to get off scot-free, and there wasn't one thing anyone could do about it.

His lawyer, at Bruce's suggestion, had dropped Daddy's name to the judge, prosecuting attorney, and anyone else that might have any say in this case. Would you want to put an ex-FBI agent, who is the son of the current Vice President of the United States, in a federal prison? That question made anyone who had any prospect of a career hesitate. Everyone agreed that what Bruce needed was to have a psychiatric evaluation and probably spend the rest of his life in some asylum, heavily guarded, but in an asylum. If Bruce could ever be rehabilitated, that would be the greatest comeback story in the world. The thought of it all made Bruce laugh even harder. He knew it was a matter of minutes before someone showed up to give him some medicine to calm him down.

He tried to settle himself down, but then he began to recall the lawyer telling him about Trip's reaction to the ruling. From what the lawyer had told Bruce, Trip nearly frothed at the mouth because he was so furious. The thought of cool, by-the-book Trip, losing it over what he had done to John made Bruce howl in laughter. Seconds later, the door opened, and a nurse, accompanied by two armed guards, appeared to give him something to make him drift off. As Bruce's mind began to wander off, all he could think was of the reckoning that was coming. Chet had shot him, and he was going to pay for that. Bruce noticed he couldn't feel his legs from the medicine, or maybe he was so high from the medicine, he couldn't. As he drifted away, he thought that would be a fair trade. Chet wasn't going to feel his legs anymore either. Now, whether or not he lived after that, Bruce hadn't quite decided yet, but Chet was never going to use his legs again. The thought made Bruce smile as he drifted off.

Archibald Staples
Virginia

Chapter 41

Archibald stood in the middle of his office, thinking about all of the hiding places he had in his home. He had checked each one twice to make sure nothing was there that could connect him to Doctor Nichols. Archibald wasn't very happy. He knew the life he led carried certain risks, and he was willing to accept them. It was when he got caught because of someone else's mistake that made him most upset. Archibald was willing to pay for any crime he committed, but he wasn't about to pay for someone else's stupidity. He sighed and tried to calm down. He thought back to the unexpected phone call he had received that morning.

Kenneth called him and had insisted that they meet at their normal spot for lunch. Archibald could hear in Kenneth's voice that this really wasn't a request. It didn't take a genius to figure out something bad had happened. With John gone, Archibald thought his biggest problems were over. Apparently, people who had been competent in the past had come down with a surprising case of the stupids!

Archibald shut his eyes to try to calm himself. He was impressed more and more by Kenneth with each passing day. In the past few weeks, he had taken tremendous personal loss, but he hadn't let that drive him from the course. No, if anything, it drove Kenneth even more. Archibald let go and let his mind drift back to the lunch he and Kenneth had just a few hours ago, and what Kenneth told him that even Archibald never would have had the courage to suggest.

Archibald Staples, a Few Hours Earlier
Private Restaurant Outside of Washington, D.C.

Chapter 42

Archibald entered the agreed upon location and went through the normal security procedures. When he sat down with his friend, he could immediately see on Kenneth's face that something was wrong. In the past few weeks, Kenneth had lost his wife and his job, but, at no point, did he look as upset as he did right now. Archibald knew this could only mean one thing. Something had gone wrong with their business, which in both men's mind was unacceptable.

"I hate to be so blunt," Kenneth began, without even a greeting. "But, circumstances dictate we forego our usual pleasantries." Archibald nodded, and Kenneth continued. He raised a cup of coffee, took a drink, placed the cup back on the saucer, and folded his hands in front of him. Clearly, whatever this was bothered Kenneth.

"I have received a phone call from a mutual friend of ours," Kenneth said, looking directly in Archibald's eyes. Archibald understood that Kenneth meant Duck. He nodded, and Kenneth continued. "My father," Kenneth paused, separated his hands, left his right arm on the table as he pulled back his left hand. He placed the hand on his leg. He looked very upset. He turned back to Archibald. "My father has screwed up," he spat out. His eyes were shooting daggers, and disgust covered Kenneth's face. Archibald knew this was very serious.

"What happened?" Archibald asked softly.

"The clinic was broken into, and a baby was stolen," Kenneth replied. It took Archibald a second to process what was said. The first thing that ran through his mind was the paperwork or evidence that might lead back to Kenneth. When the men had come up with their plans a few years ago, they all agreed that Kenneth had to be kept clean. Archibald let himself be slightly amused at that thought. There were things about Kenneth that weren't clean at all, but no one would suspect or be able to put together the puzzle. But, that was a story for another day.

"Can it be traced back to me?" Archibald asked after a few seconds of thinking. Kenneth thought for a second and barely nodded his head.

"Maybe," Kenneth admitted. Archibald thought as much.

"How much do they know?" Archibald asked.

"Not much, but enough, I'm afraid," Kenneth responded. "Right now, they are searching for the missing baby. They haven't put everything together yet, but if they should . . . my father knows better, but we both know he might talk." Archibald was nodding.

"The lawyer?" Archibald asked. Kenneth quickly shook his head no as he drank from the coffee cup. He sat down the cup.

"He thinks everything is legal," Kenneth responded. "All he knows is he connected two willing clients." Kenneth paused, reached across the table, and put his hand on Archibald's wrist, as if to make a vow. He looked Archibald directly in the eye. "If I have to, I will take care of this," Kenneth said as he let go of Archibald's wrist and leaned back in his chair. The look on Kenneth's face left no doubt exactly what Kenneth meant by his words.

Chapter 43

"Is that wise?" Archibald asked. Kenneth shrugged. It was very clear that Kenneth was furious with his father.

"He knew the risks when he entered this arrangement," Kenneth replied. He looked away a minute and stared out a window. When he turned back, anger was spread across his face. "We have kept him very comfortable. We have suggested several times that he retire or just have his practice at the hospital, but he refuses." Kenneth shook his head and continued. "He has too much of a conscience for this side job, and that will be his undoing."

Archibald sat quietly. He wasn't sure what the right answer was, but if Kenneth was willing to take care of his father for him . . . Archibald couldn't have been more proud of Kenneth if he was his own flesh and blood.

"Tell me what to do," Archibald replied, putting his well-being into his friend's hands.

"Let this play out," Kenneth said. "If they come for you, let them arrest you." Archibald nodded. "We both know no one in prison will hurt you, and I imagine we can make sure you're in a minimum security prison. Once we find out exactly what my father said, if it can be corrected by eliminating him, I'll take care of it."

"Are you sure that's wise?" Archibald asked again.

"Are you asking me if it's wise to have him killed?" Kenneth asked, a smile forming on his face. Archibald leaned close. "No one will hear us here my friend. Feel free to speak freely," Kenneth encouraged Archibald. Archibald shook his head.

"You know exactly what I'm asking," Archibald replied. "We've worked hard to keep you clean. I know that you're not. No one can put everything together, but why chance it on him?" Kenneth slammed his fist down on the table in frustration.

"That man," Kenneth began, his face red, and spittle almost flying from his mouth. "Is close to costing me the closest thing I've had to a father!"

Archibald roared with laughter at the irony. Kenneth never considered his father as anything more than a life-giver. Kenneth would rather see his own father dead than the man that he considered a father in jail. Archibald leaned back and considered what Kenneth said, and he nodded. Kenneth's anger began to dissipate some.

"Don't do anything that could get you caught," Archibald said. Kenneth smiled.

"Even if they did catch me, they can't prove it," Kenneth replied. Archibald smiled. Kenneth did have the greatest alibi in the world. Archibald just hoped they never had to test it to see if it would stand up to FBI scrutiny.

Archibald Staples
Virginia

Chapter 44

Archibald opened his eyes and looked around the room. His eyes settled on his briefcase, which contained a laptop. He walked over to the briefcase, opened it, and looked at the laptop. It was top of the line, costing several thousand dollars. He remembered he had loaded a few documents on the laptop from a flash drive of Kenneth's. He picked up the computer, raised it above his head, and brought it crashing down onto the brick fireplace. He brought it down over and over until it broke from his hands. He then began to stomp the remaining pieces until sweat covered his body. After he stopped, he turned around, out of breath. His daughter, with a few of his body guards, stood there looking at him.

"Tank," Veronica said to the large man beside her. "Make sure all of that gets picked up, and then, make sure it gets dumped in the river." She looked at her father as she said that as if to confirm this was what he wanted done. Archibald nodded. Veronica looked at him for a minute and then turned to leave. She turned back around.

"Is there something I should know?" Veronica asked. Archibald shook his head no. Veronica nodded. "Any word on David George?" she asked. Archibald shook his head no again. Veronica nodded again and began to walk into the room. "Are these outbursts normal?"

"It's none of your business what is normal and what isn't! Is that clear!?" Archibald bellowed. "If you don't like the way things are here, you are more than welcome to leave." Veronica gave Archibald a look, turned, and left. Tank acted as though he saw nothing and began to clean up the mess.

"Are you okay, Boss?" Tank asked quietly.

"I'm fine, Tank," Archibald answered just as quietly. "I may have some legal problems come up in the next few days." Tank shot his head up in surprise. Archibald continued. "I want you to run things just the way you always have." Tank nodded. He gathered all the remaining parts and left with them. Tank would make sure everything was disposed of, and it would never trace back to Archibald.

Archibald sat down in his chair. He leaned back and looked up at the ceiling. He knew all he could do now was wait. He hated waiting. Archibald smiled to himself. He got the irony of the situation. Archibald had out lasted John, but now his little gal pal was the one in charge of the investigation down in Miami. John had told Archibald that he would bring him down if it was the last thing he ever did. Well John had lied about that, but now, that girl, Jessica, might be the one to bring him in. Archibald chuckled at the thought for a second. Then he exploded, grabbed his desk, and flipped it over, throwing its contents everywhere. As everyone ran into the room to see what had happened, Archibald could only think about how much he hated incompetence.

FBI Field Office
Miami, Florida

Chapter 45

Ron and Chet began to walk back toward the FBI field office after lunch.

"That was great, Ron," Chet said, carrying a brown paper bag. Ron shrugged.

"I expect you to show me the best places in New York to eat if I ever get there," Ron responded.

"Deal," Chet said.

"Can I ask you something, Chet?" Ron asked. Chet nodded.

"Is there something wrong with you two?" Ron asked. Chet looked at Ron, confused. "You and Jessica both seem out to prove something, and I have no idea why." Chet sighed.

"Ron, for three years, Jessica and I chased one case and one case only," Chet began. "We did everything in our power to figure out who killed our friend's wife, and we couldn't solve it. Then, John returned, figured it all out, and my lack of training caused me not to properly clear a crime scene, and my friend got shot and killed." Chet paused in the story and the walk. They stood under a tree. Ron was listening intently. Chet continued.

"Jessica was on the fast track to be whatever she wanted to be. I could care less if my FBI career is over. I can find other things to do, but I love what the FBI lets me do. I get to chase conspiracies, or whatever I want. Jessica," Chet paused and shook his head. He gave a rueful smile and continued. "You have to understand, Jessica hasn't got anything else. She has to prove to her family that she can do this. She hates anyone thinking she got where she is because of her looks. She is the second best

101

agent I've ever worked with, and that's saying something. She doesn't have the God-given abilities that John does, but she is a great investigator, or detective, or whatever you want to call her. She doesn't give herself enough credit. She thought we failed John by not figuring everything out while he was gone. The truth is, only John could have, and did, figure out who killed his wife." Chet was silent, and Ron didn't have any clue what to say.

"It must be hard," Ron said after a minute or so of silence. Chet looked at him. "Losing your partner like that after all he had been through."

Chet nodded and looked away for a couple of seconds. When he looked back, there were tears in his eyes.

"Look," Chet began. "There are a lot of things about that case that I can't tell you, but I can tell you this; I let both my partners down. I don't want to do that ever again. I don't like how it made me feel, and I don't see how anyone can ever trust me again. If I'm going to be an agent, then I have to be an agent, and not just some computer junkie. Do you understand?" Ron nodded. He didn't agree with Chet, but right now, Chet didn't want to hear anything else. Chet continued. "If you could, would you not mention any of this around Jessica?" Ron nodded again and looked down the street.

"We better stop talking then," Ron said. Chet looked confused. "I believe that's your partner over there," Ron said, pointing down the street toward Jessica. Chet nodded, and in silence, the two men headed toward her.

Chapter 46

Jessica saw Ron and Chet approaching the building at the same time she was. Chet was holding a bag, and when he saw her, he grinned. He waved, sniffed the bag, and looked like he had died and gone to heaven. Jessica returned the wave and headed toward the two men.

"Jessica, I brought you lunch," Chet said as he handed her the bag. Jessica opened the bag and looked in at the sandwich. The smell made her mouth water, and her stomach made noises like some alien in a space war movie.

"What is it?" she asked. Chet smiled and hit Ron's arm with the back of his hand.

"I told you she'd love it," Chet said to Ron. He turned toward Jessica. "It's a Cuban sandwich."

"This isn't a Cuban," Jessica said. "I've had a Cuban, and they don't smell this delicious!" Ron laughed.

"The people of Tampa will tell you this is a cheap knock-off of the real thing," Ron replied. Jessica shook her head.

"We might have to go to Tampa," Jessica said to Chet, not joking. Chet laughed.

"Hey, at least you've got good pizza," Ron said. Chet stopped mid-stride, closed his eyes, and winced. Jessica sighed and turned toward Ron. Ron didn't know what he had done, but he wished he hadn't.

"Let's just say I'm not a fan," Jessica said calmly. Ron started to say something when Chet cut him off.

"Let it go man; it's not worth it," Chet said, forcefully. "Trust me; walk away man. Walk away clean." Jessica smiled a tight smile at the two and headed in the building. Ron turned to Chet after she went inside.

"What'd I do?" he asked.

"You about got hit with the Hammer," Chet replied. "Jessica thinks Chicago style is the greatest pizza ever. She has gone toe-to-toe with some lifelong residents of

Brooklyn over it . . . and won!" Chet headed inside, while Ron stood outside, shaking his head.

"These people are crazy about their food," he said out loud to no one. He sighed and headed inside after them.

Chapter 47

Jessica sat down at a chair beside the desk at which Ron had been working at. She looked at the flashing icon at the bottom of his screen. She decided it could wait a second as she pulled the sandwich out of the bag. She hoped it tasted nearly as good as it smelled. She bit into it and stifled a moan. It tasted better than it smelled, if that was possible. Chet came in and saw her.

"You okay?" he asked her. "It looks like you're having some type of experience." Ron was behind them and heard the exchange. He chuckled and began to sit down at his chair as he noticed the blinking icon on his computer. He pulled up the records quickly. Chet forgot about Jessica and her sandwich. Jessica continued to chew as she watched Ron work. She glanced down at some names Ron had jotted down on a notebook.

"Who's Emma Marcia?" Jessica asked with a mouth full of food. But, with food in her mouth it was nothing more than a bunch of mumbles. Chet turned and gave her a withered look.

"Chew," he said simply. "Emma is the nurse I interviewed today. She seemed like something was wrong when I started talking to her."

"Any relation to Felipe Marcia?" Jessica asked.

"How would I know?" Chet responded. Ron stopped mid-typing and turned toward Jessica.

"I know that name," he said and went back to work.

"What happened on the search?" Chet asked.

"One of your nurses, Sheila Long, came back having a Swiss bank account," Ron answered, never turning from the computer. He was typing furiously. Jessica had no idea what he was doing, but it did look most impressive. A photo shot up on his monitor. Jessica recognized over 70% of the people in the picture.

"Wait!" she exclaimed. "I know most of those people." Ron sat back, nodding. He was waiting on another search to complete.

"This group of guys started working together to clean up the drug trade in their area of the neighborhood. They had a leader named Oscar Lopez. Oscar was military; he was called back overseas and died a few months ago," Ron explained.

"He was also married to the lady who Dr. Nichols said had a stillbirth a few days ago," Jessica said. Ron and Chet turned toward Jessica. A beep on the computer got all three's attention. Ron leaned forward, and let out a low whistle.

"You were right, Jessica," Ron said. "Emma and Felipe are cousins."

"So, let's review what we learned," Jessica said. Both men turned towards her. "We have a group that broke into the birth clinic and stole a baby. The doctor that delivered this baby had a young lady, Christina, as a patient that had a stillbirth a few days ago. The young lady told the group of men in this picture that she brought her baby home from the hospital today. Christina had been released previously from the hospital, but the baby needed to stay for some tests. We know that she helped clean up a neighborhood from drugs, but maybe losing her husband and living in the place that they had gone to so much trouble to fight for was too much, and she turned to drugs." Jessica sat back and thought about the scenario she had just presented. It didn't feel right; something was off. Ron looked over at the two agents, appearing somewhat disappointed.

"So that's it? It's over?" he asked. Chet chuckled and shook his head.

"No," he replied simply. "There are a whole lot of unanswered questions out there, like where is the baby?" Jessica nodded.

"I'm just throwing what we know out there and seeing how it fits together," Jessica said to Ron. "We don't know if what Felipe and his crew told us is true. We're a long ways from solving this one. I'd love to know what Sheila Long is doing with a Swiss bank account. I mean, it's not illegal, but it does raise some eyebrows. I need to talk to her and the Williamses. What about Emma Marcia?" Jessica asked, turning toward Chet. Chet frowned.

"Something was off," Chet admitted. "She knows something, but I think she's scared. I don't think taking a run at her right now will pay off. We might try the others, and if we come up empty, come back at her." Jessica nodded.

"Sounds like a plan," she said, standing. "Ron, why don't you drive since you know Miami better than us?" Ron looked pleasantly surprised to be allowed to join in.

"Really?" he asked. Jessica nodded. "Thanks guys!" Ron took off toward the door. Chet held back to talk to Jessica.

"You called him," Chet said, not asked. Jessica nodded. "He said you were doing everything the way he would?" Jessica nodded. Chet smiled and looked Jessica right in her eyes. "Good, now listen to him and quit doubting yourself!" Chet turned and walked after Ron like he had just proven something. Jessica shook her head and followed the two men to the car.

Chapter 48

The three rode in silence to the hospital. Ron was concentrating on driving in traffic, Chet was on his cellphone checking who knew what, and Jessica was thinking about the case. Something was very off about the entire case. Jessica couldn't put her finger on what was bugging her. She thought for a minute and decided there was something about the crime scene photos that bothered her. She pulled the photos out of the envelope she was carrying them in and began to study them. One of the video tapes had captured Mrs. Williams screaming at the thieves to give her back her baby. Jessica studied the picture, not sure what was bothering her. Jessica knew from the report that the Williamses were very, very well-to-do. She looked the part of the rich housewife. She was thin and fit; her hair seemed to be in great shape, like she had just stepped out of a salon. Despair shown on her slim face from her baby being kidnapped.

"I thought pregnant women shouldn't get perms," Jessica muttered.

"That's actually a myth," Ron responded. Chet looked up from the back seat. He and Jessica shared a look of surprise. Ron didn't notice and continued. "The fumes don't hurt the babies. Many hairstylists won't perm pregnant ladies' hair because with all the hormones in their body, the perm doesn't do what it is supposed to." Ron finally realized both Chet and Jessica were staring at him. "I had an aunt who was a hairstylist," he admitted.

'I'm sorry, Ron," Jessica said. "It's just that I'm not use to getting hair facts from our third party. If you had told us the use of a 2-3 zone, then that would be the norm. It took both of us off guard." Jessica flipped back through the pictures and stopped. The picture was of one of the thieves carrying the baby. The person was cradling the baby. It seemed almost motherly to Jessica. It fit what they had been told by the nurse at the clinic. It was this picture that made her feel uneasy.

"Chet, anything come back unusual on the birth at the clinic from the lab?" she asked, knowing this was a reach. Ron had a bewildered look on his face, as did Chet.

"What are you talking about, Jessica?" Chet asked. Now, the feeling in her gut was growing. She thought she knew what had happened, but it was going to be very hard to prove it. Jessica flipped to the next picture, and all doubts of what happened were pushed from her mind.

"Chet, two things," Jessica began. "I want a subpoena for all records on Carrie Williams. Why she was under the care of Dr. Nichols? Secondly, I want this picture blown up." She handed the picture she had been looking at to Chet. The kidnapper was looking up at the camera while holding the baby.

"Jess, how do you expect me to get a judge to sign off on medical records? Chet asked.

"You tell the judge that a child has been kidnapped and we're trying to exhaust every possible angle to find the child," she snapped. Chet jumped a little at her outburst.

"I'm sorry," Jessica answered. "I just think the answer to our questions may lie in her records." Chet nodded, and the three continued on in silence to the hospital.

Chapter 49

The three agents entered the hospital on a mission. Chet was on the phone with a judge, trying to get a warrant. It sounded to Jessica like he was succeeding. The judge was just leery about issuing a warrant for medical records, but it was possible the life of a baby was at stake. Jessica had always heard that nothing moved judges into action more than the lives of babies or children being in danger. She let Chet deal with the judge as she and Ron navigated their way through the hospital to find Sheila Long.

Jessica flashed her badge when she needed to, but for the most part, no one seemed to stop the three. Jessica wasn't sure if it was the looks on their faces or the fact that these doctors, nurses, and techs were so overworked and understaffed. Jessica imagined it was a combination of the two. They entered the pediatric ward. Jessica walked right up to the front desk. She pulled out her badge and laid it on the counter in front of her.

"My name is Jessica Hammerstein with the FBI," she said to the lady working the desk. She wasn't sure what the woman's rank was she was talking to, but Jessica didn't care. "I have to see nurse Sheila Long right now." The woman started to open her mouth to say something. Jessica had been doing her job long enough to know that she wasn't about to tell her where Sheila was but instead some excuse. Jessica shut her down before she ever got started. "I don't care what it is you're about to tell me. I don't care what she is doing, unless it is physically saving a life right this second. A baby has been kidnapped, and she may know something to help me find that infant. That's all I care about. Are we clear?" The person in front of her nodded and pointed down the hall.

"There is a lounge down there," the person said. Jessica nodded, grabbed her badge, and the three began marching down the hallway. She came to the door that said Authorized Personnel only. Jessica opened the door and walked in. A lady in nurse's scrubs sat at the table. She looked up at Jessica and started to say something but stopped when she saw the look on Jessica's face.

"Sheila Long?" Jessica asked. The lady nodded. "I'm Jessica Hammerstein, this is Ronald McGuire, and that is Chet Morris. We're all agents with the FBI. I need to ask you a few questions." Sheila nodded. Chet was still arguing on the phone with the judge. He was loud enough that Sheila could hear him.

"May I ask what he is doing?" Sheila asked, pointing at Chet.

"He's attempting to get a warrant for the files on Carrie Williams that Dr. Nichols has on her," Jessica replied. Sheila smiled and chuckled.

"You can tell him to stop anytime," Sheila responded. Jessica was shocked. She had never seen someone in the medical field just turn over files before. She understood why they didn't; there were federal laws against it. Sheila continued. "There are no files on Carrie Williams for Dr. Nichols." Jessica reached down and grabbed the chair in front of her. She wasn't shocked with what Sheila said; she was shocked that evidence was starting to support what she believed.

Chapter 50

"What exactly do you mean that there isn't a file on Carrie Williams?" a shocked Chet asked. Sheila chuckled and shrugged.

"There isn't any file on Carrie Williams," she said matter-of-factly. "I have never heard of that patient in my life, and I am Dr. Nichols's personal nurse. I know all of the patients that go and deliver at that clinic, and I know all of the patients that deliver at the hospital. What I'm trying to tell you, for whatever reason, the Williamses either decided or were referred to Dr. Nichols at the last second. There is no history with that patient."

Jessica nodded her head. She decided on a different approach.

"What can you tell me about Christina Lopez?" Jessica asked. Sheila's face flickered something for just a second. Jessica didn't catch it, and she really wished John had been here, but he wasn't. There was distain on her face as she talked about Christina.

"That girl," she began. Sheila stopped and shook her head. "All she had to do was tell Dr. Nichols what she had been taking, or doing, and he could have prevented the horrible death." Jessica nodded.

"Have there been any other baby deaths in the past month or so?" Jessica asked. Sheila paused for a second. She looked at Jessica, not sure what to say. "If there are, please tell me. This could be connected to the case." Sheila looked a little uncomfortable, but began to talk.

"There was this girl about four weeks ago," Sheila began. "She was, oh, how do I put this delicately? She worked the streets," Sheila offered up. Jessica nodded for her to continue. "I don't know what exactly happened, but it shook Dr. Nichols up pretty badly. He was nearly beside himself. Either the girl had decided that eight months of pregnancy was enough, or her pimp did, or someone did. Do you understand what I'm saying?" Jessica did; she nodded, urging her to continue. "After that, Dr. Nichols seemed, I don't know, worried? I'm not for sure why he got so upset. I mean, it's terrible that child was carried to eight months, but we were all prepared for the worst case scenario. Even Dr. Nichols admitted it would be a miracle if this baby survived."

"I thought he was the best at those with high-risk pregnancies?" Jessica asked.

"Well, sure," Sheila replied. "He's great when there are diseases, or some genetic condition involved. He's one of the best, but you can't save the ones that abuse drugs and alcohol. He deals with those cases when others just won't. Everyone knows that if there is a high-risk, he can beat the odds. But no one, and I mean no one, can help it when the mother continually abuses her body."

"So most of the babies he loses that are considered normal pregnancies really aren't?" Jessica asked. Sheila nodded.

"It's only after the fact when we learn all the reasons why the child died that we find out it's a high-risk pregnancy," Sheila said, looking proud.

"That makes sense," Jessica responded. "Explain to me something that doesn't make sense to me. At the crime scene this morning, there was no evidence of a delivery of a baby," Jessica said to Sheila who looked confused.

"What do you mean that there was no evidence of a delivery," Sheila said. "If there was a birth, there was evidence. It's not a neat and tidy process! Catherine probably cleaned up everything before you got there."

Jessica thought for a second. There was nothing else she needed out of Sheila. It was time for her to talk to her about the inconsistencies of her stories with other testimony.

"Thank you, Sheila," Jessica began. Sheila smiled, and Jessica pressed on. "But, you see, I have a problem. Actually, I have many problems. First off, how did you know Catherine was at the scene? I never mentioned her name. Secondly, everyone that personally knows Christina says that she isn't a drug user, and furthermore, her baby didn't die but came home from the hospital this morning. So, I have to figure out who's lying, the people that know Christina or you," Jessica paused and then leaned in very close. "Personally, I think it's you."

Chapter 51

"I don't know who you think you are," Sheila began, but Jessica was having none of it and cut her off by slamming her hand down on the table, fire blazing in her eyes.

"I'll tell you exactly who I am, missy," Jessica said fiercely, but quietly, staring into Sheila's eyes. "I am Jessica Hammerstein, and they call me the Hammer in the FBI because of my ability in the interrogation box. Now, if you don't answer my questions truthfully, I have no problem slapping cuffs on you, dragging you through this hospital in front of all your coworkers, and throwing you into a box where I will perform surgery on you that there is no recovery from. Do we understand each other?" Jessica asked. There was no answer for a second, and Jessica slammed her hand down on the table again. "DO WE!?" Sheila nodded vigorously. Jessica straightened up, when she did, she saw the look of shock on Ron's face; she glanced at Chet, who was trying hard to keep a straight face. Jessica suppressed a smile and began.

"How do you know about Catherine?" Jessica said calmly.

"She's Dr. Nichols right-hand woman at the clinic, for lack of a better term," Sheila answered. "She does everything over there that I do over here. She makes sure everything runs like clockwork. I didn't know that she was there, but it only makes sense to me. They are so understaffed over there that Catherine would do whatever was necessary. If anyone cleaned that room up, it was her."

"She wasn't there when the baby was delivered," Jessica said.

"I wasn't either, so I don't know," Sheila replied.

"OK, so if Catherine didn't do it, is there anyone else who would?" Jessica asked. Sheila shook her head.

"I don't know for sure, but I doubt it," Sheila replied.

"Ok, how do you explain how a woman who spends her entire life fighting drug pushers and cleaning up the block she lives on, gives in to the very thing she is fighting?" Jessica asked.

"Lady, I can't answer that question," Sheila responded. "You have to understand that none of us truly knows why someone takes drugs. If I'm not mistaken, she lost her husband, the man that helped her clean up that block." Jessica nodded. "Think about this. If everywhere you turned reminded you of the man you loved, if everything you did in your job reminded you of the man you lost, of the love of your life, do you think you'd be strong enough to carry on the fight by yourself, or do you think you might slip? Then, think about this. If one of those drug pushers figured the same thing out, do you think they would be above approaching her at her darkest hour? Would you be strong enough to say no? Would you?" Sheila was looking Jessica directly in the eye.

Jessica thought her heart was going to break in two. She would be in that exact scenario if John had really died. She saw what John went through with Sam's death. She wasn't entirely sure what she would do in that situation. She felt Chet at her side. She looked over at him and flashed him a smile to let him know she was all right.

"Ok," Jessica said, trying to get this conversation back on track. "Did you see the Lopez child die?"

"I didn't, but I was there when Dr. Nichols called it," Sheila answered, looking down at the floor. She looked back up at Jessica. "Look, I'm not trying to be uncooperative, but I do have patients on this floor."

"Fair enough," Jessica responded. "But I'm going to talk to some of the nurses." Sheila knew it wasn't a question and nodded to show she wasn't going to put up a fight.

"One last question," Jessica said. "What about your Swiss bank account?" Sheila shrugged.

"Is that illegal?" Sheila asked. Jessica shook her head no. "Then, it's none of your business." Sheila got up and left the room without another word. Jessica didn't think pursuing it right now would do any good. What Sheila had said about Oscar had hit home with Jessica, and she really didn't have it in her to drag information out of her about the account. Besides, she would have Chet do some more research and come back at her at a later time. She turned and saw Ron looking at her, worried.

"Are you all right?" Ron asked Jessica. Jessica smiled at Ron.

"Yeah," she replied. "Sometimes it's like he's never left, you know what I mean?" Ron smiled. "Could you go find Emma for us?" Ron nodded and left the room.

"It's like he never left us?" Chet asked, snickering. Jessica turned toward Chet, fighting the smile on her face.

"You can never tell him any of this," Jessica said. "He'll never let any of us live this down." Chet nodded, laughing.

"That's the last thing his ego needs," Chet replied. They both tried to stop the laughter as the door handle turned, and Ron led in another nurse that Jessica could only assume was Emma Marcia.

Chapter 52

Ron led the nurse in and had her take a seat. Jessica came over, shook her hand, and sat down at the table with her.

"Emma?" Jessica asked. Emma nodded. "First off," Jessica began. "You're not in any trouble. I'm Jessica Hammerstein with the FBI, and this is Ron," Jessica said, gesturing toward Ron. "The man over there, you should have talked to earlier today, Chet." Chet gave a friendly wave. "I need to ask you questions about Christina Lopez."

"I told Chet that I didn't know anything earlier," Emma said. Jessica nodded.

"Emma," Jessica began. "I met a young man today named Felipe." Jessica paused and watched Emma's face. Emma didn't give anything away. Jessica continued. "I have pictures of the men that kidnapped the Williamses' baby, and I really think that Felipe is one of those men." Jessica watched Emma very closely as she spoke. Jessica could have sworn that anger flashed in Emma's eyes when she said the Williamses' baby.

"Felipe wouldn't kidnap anyone!" Emma exclaimed. "He's a good boy! He helped Christina and Oscar clean up that neighborhood. Do you know how proud our family is of him, and how much we appreciate Christina and Oscar for what they did?"

Jessica sat there for a minute and looked over at Ron and Chet. Jessica was almost 100% positive of what was going on, but she was afraid that Emma would never tell what happened unless it was just the two of them.

"Hang on a second," Jessica said. She got up and walked over to the two men. "Can I see you two outside for a minute?" The two men nodded and followed her outside.

"What's up?" Chet asked.

"She knows something, but she's never going to say it in front of you two," Jessica began. "Furthermore, I don't think she'll ever tell what happened in a courtroom, if it gets that far." Chet and Ron nodded. "We agree the important thing right now is getting the child back, right?" Both men nodded again. "Then let me talk to her, just the two of us."

"Fine with me, Boss," Chet said. Jessica looked a little taken aback and smiled.

"Boss?" she asked.

"Boss," Chet repeated.

"You understand I can't tell you what we talk about," Jessica said. Ron started to object, but Chet put his hand on Ron's shoulder. Ron looked at Chet.

"Trust us," Chet said. Ron didn't look happy, but he nodded and relented.

"You'll find the baby?" Chet asked.

"I'm almost positive," Jessica replied. Chet nodded, and Jessica turned and went back into the room, while Chet and Ron made sure she had her privacy. After fifteen minutes, Jessica came back with a determined look on her face.

"Well?" Chet asked.

"I think I know exactly what happened, but proving it? That's going to be rough," she said. "Can you get someone to keep an eye on Sheila and pick her up if need be?" Chet nodded.

"Is the baby okay?" Chet asked. Jessica smiled and nodded.

"If I'm right, the baby couldn't be safer," Jessica said, beginning to walk down the hall. Chet and Ron began to chase after her.

"Is it always like this?" Ron asked. Chet shook his head no and began to make a phone call to get someone to tail Sheila.

119

"Oh, no," he replied. "Usually, it's me and Jessica chasing after John."

Chapter 53

"Where to?" Ron asked when they reached the car. Jessica thought for a second and decided it was time to go to the Williamses' home. Ron navigated the streets, and within fifteen minutes, they were at the address they had found on file. Jessica noticed they were in a very upscale neighborhood. The house they pulled up in front of was easily over three thousand square feet if not larger. Jessica really wasn't for sure since all she had to compare it to was her apartment in New York. She knew it wasn't as big as the sprawling house the Moores owned, but exactly how it compared, she wasn't for sure.

Chet and Ron led the way, and Jessica held back. She had seen John pull this trick many times. John would always observe, and when he saw things were going a way he didn't want or wanted to push the questioning in a certain way, only then would he get involved. Jessica was starting to understand that philosophy. The Williamses seemed very helpful. They offered to let the agents search the entire house. Jessica listened to the attempt Chet and Ron were making at casual conversation with the couple. For some reason, Jessica had it in her mind that the two had been coached on what to say. Jessica couldn't put her finger on it, but her gut was telling her that that was what was going on. John had always told her that her gut feelings were actually her mind putting things together that she hadn't yet consciously connected. Plus, with what Emma had told her, that would make a great deal of sense.

Jessica excused herself to go to the restroom and took an unsupervised look around the house. She was snooping in the back part of the house when she found the laundry room and the lady who was apparently the maid of the house.

"I'm sorry," Jessica said. The housekeeper looked a little surprised. "I'm with the FBI," Jessica said, showing her badge. The maid relaxed and went back to her work.

Jessica noticed that the maid was washing his and her track suits. "Do both of the Williamses run?" she asked.

"Oh, yes," the maid responded. "Mrs. Williams got Mr. Williams to start running with her a few years ago, and he has dropped a lot of weight."

"That's good," Jessica replied, looking at the track suits. Something was bothering her about them. "Too many men don't take their health seriously." The maid nodded. She leaned in close as if to tell Jessica a secret.

"Mrs. Williams has to get both of them out the door each morning for their workout, or Mr. Williams would never run," she said in a very low voice.

"Men," Jessica responded, while shaking her head. They shared a chuckle. Jessica leaned against the door frame and thought about what the housekeeper had said. "Every day? She has to make him run every day?" Jessica was shaking her head disapprovingly as she spoke. The maid nodded with the same disapproving look.

"You would think in her condition that he would put forth more of an effort," the maid said. Jessica nodded as the realization of how she would prove what she thought was going on hit her like a ton of bricks.

"Is there anyone you could think of that might want to hurt either of your employers?" Jessica asked. The maid shook her head. "Is there anything hidden in their room that might give me a clue?" The maid gave her a look. Jessica leaned in. "I know if anyone knows, you do." The housekeeper smiled at Jessica.

"You are more than welcome to look through their room," the maid replied. "It's at the top of the stairs." Jessica thanked the lady and headed up the stairs. She found the room and started checking the closet. She found Carrie's side and began looking through the clothes. All the tags on the clothes ran a size 4. Jessica returned everything the way it was and headed back down the stairs. It was time she questioned the Williamses.

Chapter 54

Jessica made her way back to the main room where Chet and Ron were still talking to the Williamses. It was clear that Chet and Ron had just about run out of things to say with the relief their faces showed when she appeared.

"Okay, boys," Jessica said, smiling at her two partners. "I need a favor again." Ron looked at her suspiciously, and Chet chuckled.

"Want us to leave you alone with these two?" Ron asked. Jessica beamed at him.

"That's a great idea," Jessica said. "While you're at it, will you tell the person tailing Sheila that we're going to have to arrest her?" Jessica watched the Williamses out of the corner of her eye while she was talking to the two. Mark swallowed visibly, and Carrie looked like someone had punched her in the gut. Jessica was thrilled with the reaction. Ron had an eyebrow raised in surprise at Jessica, but she kept going.

"We probably need to find out exactly where Dr. Nichols is as well," she continued. "We're also going to arrest him."

"What's the charge?" Ron asked, amazed. Jessica frowned and tapped her finger on her lip.

"Let's go with accessory to kidnapping for now," she replied, looking over at the Williamses. "When I finish talking to these two, I'll know if we need to bring in a wagon or not for Mark and Carrie." Carrie was near tears, and Mark was as white as a ghost. Jessica knew she had all but tied a bow on this case.

"You two head out, and I'll take care of them," she said gently, but firmly.

Ron and Chet headed outside. Ron was shaking his head the entire way. When they got outside, Ron turned to Chet.

"What is going on?" he demanded from Chet.

123

"Calm down," Chet said. "This is nothing against you or me. She's trying to scare those two into confessing, and from the looks on their faces, they are in there telling her everything she wants to know."

"It's a scare tactic?" Ron asked. Chet nodded.

"Emma wasn't going to talk to you or me," Chet said, and Ron begrudgingly agreed. "These two know something and Jessica is just trying to put the fear of God into them." Ron began to chuckle and then to laugh loudly.

"You're telling me she's bluffing them?" he asked through the laughter. Chet nodded. The two made the phone calls Jessica asked, and a few minutes later, she appeared on the front porch with a satisfied look on her face.

"You two want to know what happened, or do you want to see the main event and be surprised?" Jessica asked, almost directed at Ron. Ron shook his head and smiled.

"I've been along for the ride this far; I'm ready to see the ending, spoiler free," he replied. Jessica smiled.

"Then, have everyone pick up their target, and bring them to the field office," Jessica responded. She started toward the car and then stopped. She turned on the balls of her feet with one finger up in the air, like she had forgotten something.

"Ron, do you know where I can find a woman's track suit?" she asked. Ron nodded, confused. Jessica grinned. "If you would, you two take me back to the field office so I can start interrogating Sheila. You two have an errand to run," Jessica said, her grin growing. Both Chet and Ron looked amused. Jessica continued. "We're going to need a prop for the big finish."

FBI Field Office
Miami, Florida

Chapter 55

Jessica, Chet, and Ron stood in the observation room just watching Doctor Nichols. Chet handed Jessica an envelope.

"You wanted this picture blown up," Chet reminded her. Jessica pulled out the picture and stared at it for a few seconds. She looked over at Ron.

"Can you access that photo you showed me earlier that I recognized many of the people in?" she asked. Ron nodded. He walked over to a computer, typed a few things, and the photo pulled up. Jessica looked at it for a second and then at the one in her hand. What she saw confirmed everything. Jessica turned to the two men.

"Okay, Chet," she said. "If you will hand me the package, I guess I'm ready to begin." Chet smiled and handed her the pictures of the woman's track suit they had just bought. Jessica stuck something on one of the pictures, put them in the envelope, and straightened up. "Wish me luck," she said and headed out the door.

"Like you'll need it," Chet said. Jessica flashed him a smile and headed into the hallway.

Jessica walked into the interrogation room a second later, looking deadly serious. She came in without saying a word and sat down in front of Doctor Nichols. She stared at him for a solid minute, never uttering a sound. In the observation room, Ronald McGuire leaned over to Chet.

"What is she doing?" he asked quietly, as if the two in the other room could hear him. Chet smiled and turned toward Ron.

"She's making him sweat," Chet replied. Another minute passed, and Jessica continued to say nothing.

"How long is she going to do this?" Ron asked, getting somewhat uncomfortable himself. Chet shrugged.

"You know, I don't know," he replied honestly. "Most of the time we're dealing with professionals, but this guy is a doctor. He might give it up any second. Just watch; you'll never learn this in any class." Ron watched. The doctor looked like he wanted to bolt out of the room. He was chewing on one fingernail, and Ron swore that more beads of sweat were popping off of the doctor's head. Jessica had the temperature in the room set on 78. She didn't seem to be warm at all, but Dr. Nichols was covered in a sheen of sweat. Jessica still didn't say a word. She opened a manila folder and pulled out the photographs inside. The pictures were of a woman's track suit that Jessica had just gotten from Chet. There was a sticky note on the picture that only read Carrie on it. Chet looked perplexed.

"What's going on?" Ron asked. Chet shrugged his shoulders.

"I honestly have no idea," Chet answered. He held up his hand to be quiet; Jessica was getting ready to speak.

"DNA," Jessica said. She was toying with the edge of the photo with the sticky note on it, while Dr. Nichols continued to chew on his fingernail. Jessica was smiling inside. This was her element. She had nothing on the doctor that was concrete, but she was pretty sure what was going on from her earlier interviews. This was her best shot of finding out she was correct and saving the child. She looked the doctor right in the eye.

"We're going to find the child," she said, quietly but forcefully. The doctor involuntarily gulped. Jessica knew she had hit a grand slam. She leaned back in her chair, her arms spread apart. "You know, I don't even have to do this." She crossed her arms and stared right into the doctor's eyes. "We both know, don't we?" If it was even possible, more sweat popped off the doctor's head.

"What in the world is she talking about?" Ron asked. Chet shook his head, confused. He was trying to put all the pieces together. He was staring at the photograph on the table in the interview room. Suddenly, it clicked. He turned to Ron, a smile crossing his face.

"Ron," Chet began. "You might want to sit down." Ron looked at Chet surprised.

"Why?" Ron asked.

"Because we're wrong about the baby kidnapping," Chet replied.

"What do you mean?" Ron asked. Chet smiled and turned back to the window.

"Just watch, buddy, just watch," Chet replied.

Chapter 56

Jessica got up out of her chair without saying a word. She gathered the pictures, put them back in the envelope, and began to head to the door.

"Where are you going?" the doctor asked. Jessica stopped walking, turned toward the doctor, and shrugged.

"What does it matter?" she asked. "I know what happened, and I don't need you," she replied as she turned and headed back toward the door.

"Wait," Brian said, jumping up out of his chair. Jessica stopped and waited. He looked down at the ground as if to gather his courage. He looked back at Jessica who had her back to him, her hand on the door ready to leave. "You've got to protect me, or he'll have me killed. I can give him to you." Jessica smiled while facing the door. She turned her head where only Chet could see the look on her face. Chet clapped his hands together in celebration. Jessica steadied the steely look on her face and turned back toward Brian.

"Who?" she asked quietly. "Who are you going to give me?"

"Archibald," the doctor said quietly. "Archibald Staples, but you've got to give me immunity and protection." Jessica stared at the doctor. "He'll kill me if you don't," he insisted. Jessica nodded slowly for fear she might leap in celebration.

"Let me make some phone calls," she responded. The doctor nodded and sat back down. Jessica calmly gathered herself and headed out the door. She shut the door, looked around, and when she saw no one was watching, did a quiet victory dance. She walked down the hall and opened the door to the observation room. She walked in and was surprised when Chet caught her in a bear hug.

"We got him Jessica; it was brilliant!" Chet exclaimed. Jessica was trying to get her breath back from the hug.

"Does someone mind filling me in?" Ron asked. Jessica winked at him and held up one finger as she called Trip. Trip picked up after the second ring.

"Trip," Jessica began. "I have someone here who says he wants to testify against Archibald Staples for immunity and protection."

"What!?" Trip exclaimed. "Is this legit, Jessica?"

"I'm pretty sure, sir," Jessica replied. "How would you like me to proceed?" There was a pause, and Jessica could just picture Trip looking at his watch.

"I'll be there in a few hours," Trip replied.

"Okay, sir," she replied. "I'll keep him prepped for you."

"You do that, Jessica," Trip said. "And, Jessica."

"Yes, sir?" she replied.

"Good job, Agent," Trip said and then disconnected. Jessica beamed and looked at Chet.

"Figure it out?" she asked Chet. Chet smiled and nodded. Ron shook his head.

"I have no idea," Ron told them.

"I get why John enjoys it," Jessica said. Chet smiled. Jessica turned back toward the window and looked in at the doctor. She had him. She had figured it out, and in the process, she was about to bring down Archibald. Now that was what she called a good day.

Chapter 57

A few hours later, Trip strolled into the interrogation area with an attorney that Jessica could only assume was with the Department of Justice. Trip and Jessica talked for a few minutes, and Trip's mouth dropped in shock. The attorney looked impressed, but shook his head at the two. Trip sent Jessica down the hallway. From the other side of the interrogation area, she could hear Trip yelling at the attorney. Things sounded like they were beginning to get very heated. After a few minutes, there was silence. Jessica heard a phone being dialed and Trip talking to someone. After a minute, she didn't hear Trip's voice any longer. She heard another voice; she could only assume it was the attorney with the Department of Justice. After a second, Jessica heard hands clapping together, and Trip appeared in the hallway with the biggest smile on his face. The attorney was following behind on the phone with someone. It appeared by his reactions he was being dressed down by whomever he was on the phone with. Jessica had a feeling Trip had used a little bit of the political pull he had, namely Jeremiah Cosby.

"It's your show, Agent," Trip said, looking like a kid on Christmas morning. Jessica smiled, waited for the attorney to end the call, and led the two men into the room where Dr. Brian Nichols was waiting. As the group filed in, Jessica watched the doctor's face. It was apparent he was wrestling with what he was about to do. The attorney began.

"Dr. Nichols, I am James with the United States Attorney's office," the attorney stated. "The Department of Justice is willing to give you full immunity for any crimes you are involved with and enter you into witness protection, as long as you agree to tell us the involvement of Archibald Staples in this case. Do you understand?" Dr. Nichols nodded. "I need that verbalized, sir," the attorney said.

"Yes," Dr. Nichols responded.

"Do you want a lawyer present?" the attorney asked.

"No," Brian said clearly. The attorney nodded and looked over at Jessica. Jessica cleared her throat and began.

"If you want a deal, Doctor, then I have the men that can give it to you, but you'll need to tell us everything," Jessica said. Brian nodded.

"What exactly do you want to know?" Brian asked.

"We want to know what you know about Archibald and what you have to do with this kidnapping case," Trip replied. Jessica smiled and turned toward Trip and the attorney.

"Guys, I'm sorry," Jessica began, smiling like the cat who caught the canary. "I forgot to mention on the phone; this isn't a kidnapping case." Both men looked stunned and confused.

"What do you mean, Jessica?" Trip asked, getting upset by the second. Jessica continued to smile.

"See, what actually happened here is the baby is back with its rightful mother," Jessica said, watching the shock cover both men's faces. Brian was slowly nodding in agreement. "What actually happened in the clinic was that a group of people led by the child's mother took the baby back and stopped the child from being sold to another couple." Jessica gave it a second to let that sink in, and then, she dropped the bomb. "And, unless I'm wrong, which I really don't think I am, the whole operation to sell the baby was financed by Archibald Staples."

Jessica and Emma
Earlier in the Nurses Break Room

Chapter 58

Jessica came back into the break room by herself. She noticed that Emma seemed more comfortable when it was just the two of them. Jessica sat back down and watched Emma for a second. If Jessica was right, what Emma did could cost Emma her job.

"Emma, let's just talk for a second," Jessica said. Emma just looked at Jessica, remaining silent. Jessica continued. "Here's the way I see it. I'm after two things. The first is getting the baby back to its parents, no matter who the parents are. The second is to find out who is the kidnapper and get them off the streets, no matter who they are." Emma absently played with her hair and just looked at Jessica.

"The way you said that," Emma began. She paused for a second, looked at Jessica, gathered her courage, and continued. "It sounds like you're not for sure who the kidnapper was." Jessica shrugged.

"Maybe things aren't the way they appeared in that video," Jessica offered. Emma didn't say anything, but she did lean forward to listen better. Jessica continued. "Maybe, and I'm just speculating here, maybe the kidnapper isn't actually in the video. Maybe that baby isn't really the Williamses' baby. I mean there is no evidence of a birth of that child, or any child that night from the birthing center." Jessica sat there, just looking at Emma. Emma chewed her bottom lip for a second, not sure what to say. After a second, she spoke softly.

"The problem with that is someone's baby was taken that night," Emma said. Jessica nodded.

132

"But was the baby taken or taken back?" Jessica asked. Emma continued to chew her bottom lip and play with her hair. Jessica leaned in slowly. "Was the group of people on the video kidnapping that baby or freeing the baby from its captors?"

Emma looked about as uncomfortable as a person could look. She glanced at Jessica several times, and finally spoke, barely above a whisper.

"Let's say that the baby was freed from its captors; how could you prove it?" Emma asked.

"DNA," Jessica said simply. "We do a DNA test on the Williamses and whoever was on that video." Emma looked down at the ground and spoke so quietly that Jessica could barely hear her.

"What if there were legal documents of the parent giving up the baby?" Emma asked. Jessica hadn't thought of that.

"I don't know," Jessica admitted. "Have you seen any such legal documents?"

"Maybe," Emma admitted. "Maybe I've seen some adoptions arranged."

"Is that what happened here?" Jessica asked. Emma didn't speak for a minute, and when she did, once again, it was very quiet.

"What happens if the baby that was supposed to be adopted dies?" Emma asked.

"I don't know the legal system that well," Jessica admitted. "But, I would think that if the baby died, then there was no deal."

"What if someone had already spent the money made on the deal?" Emma asked, and with that, Jessica finally figured out what the motive was in the kidnapping.

Chapter 59

"Sheila told me about a baby that died a few weeks ago that really upset Dr. Nichols," Jessica said to Emma. "Is that why Dr. Nichols was so upset? Did Dr. Nichols have a deal in place to have the baby adopted by the Williamses and it died? Did Dr. Nichols already spend the money from that adoption? Emma, please, I need help here." Emma had tears streaming from her eyes. Jessica was pleading with Emma. Emma slowly nodded her head. Now, it all made sense.

"Emma, that baby that died shortly after it was born here three days ago," Jessica began, but had to stop because Emma burst out in tears. Jessica enjoyed ripping people apart that did things for their own evil reasons, or those that were truly deserving of it. Emma didn't fit that profile. Jessica didn't know for sure, but she felt that Emma's job may hinge on her not telling the truth.

"Have they threatened you, Emma?" Jessica asked. Emma nodded. "Do you have kids, Emma?" Emma nodded again and held up two fingers. "Is there anyone else in your life?" Emma nearly burst into tears as she shook her head no. Jessica didn't know who had threatened Emma, but she had a pretty good idea. Jessica was ready to walk out the door, grab Sheila Long by her hair, drag her to the ground, and show her everything she learned in MMA about ground and pound. Jessica got control of herself.

"Emma, you have my word anything you say in here won't get back to Sheila or Dr. Nichols," Jessica said to her as comfortingly as she could. Emma smiled an appreciative smile at her. Emma looked back down at the floor and spoke very softly.

"The baby didn't die three days ago," she said, barely above a whisper. Jessica wanted to celebrate. This was no longer a kidnapping, and she didn't have to worry about the baby any longer. She now needed to find out if

Dr. Nichols had done anything else and who else was involved. She could only pray it somehow led back to Archibald. She had no proof, but she had to wonder, given their history of knowing each other. Emma began talking again.

"I knew Christina, but she didn't know me. Felipe is my cousin, and he was part of the group that Oscar put together to clean up his neighborhood. Our whole family is so thankful for Christina and Oscar for getting Felipe to make something of himself. When I found out it was Christina's baby that died, I was just devastated. I didn't mean to, but I stumbled across the baby in one of the back offices that wasn't being used. When I asked Sheila about it, she told me that if I said anything, I would be fired, and Dr. Nichols would give me a bad recommendation to every doctor he could. I just get by as it is, and if that happened," Emma trailed off, tears in her eyes. She took a second to gather herself. She looked up at Jessica with tears in her eyes. "I told Felipe what happened. It was because of me that they raided that birthing center."

Chapter 60

"Did you see anything that showed it was actually Christina's baby?" Jessica asked. Emma shook her head no.

"All the identifying tags had been taken off the baby," Emma replied.

"So how do you know for sure that the baby is Christina's?" Jessica asked.

"I started listening where I could, and I figured out what was going on," Emma said. She seemed to want to get out everything she was holding in, and Jessica was going to let her. "When I broke down when Sheila threatened me, she told me what had happened." Jessica could hardly contain her excitement over this revelation.

"Apparently Dr. Nichols had picked out this former prostitute to give her baby up for adoption. It was going to be a straight forward adoption as far as the prostitute knew, but Dr. Nichols was paid to have it arranged. The prostitute had no idea that money was exchanging hands. Dr. Nichols apparently had already spent the money when the prostitute came in a few weeks ago. That was when he learned that she lost the baby. Dr. Nichols freaked out, and didn't know what to do. I put some of this together from what I saw happen, so it may not be exactly right." Jessica nodded and held her breath, hoping that she would name someone else who would be involved. Jessica didn't know why she was kidding herself; she was praying it was Archibald.

"Apparently, there was a lawyer involved, and someone who had taken care of the lawyer fees. Apparently, the lawyer was paid to send people to the doctor when they didn't want to go through the proper channels for an adoption and were willing to pay to speed things up. The person who paid the lawyer some money expected that money back plus a lot more," Emma said. Jessica knew this made sense. Emma continued.

"Apparently, they decided now that everything had gone wrong, the only way to make everything work was to fake a death and have the baby be 'born' to the couple. Dr. Nichols thought that Christina fit the mold. She was a single mother that came from a historically known drug area. Dr. Nichols thought that Christina would never question anything and actually be grateful that she didn't have to 'worry about a baby'," Emma said.

"He said that?" Jessica asked.

"Sheila said he did," Emma responded. Jessica was livid.

"Why would Sheila tell you all of this?" Jessica asked.

"She thought I would feel sorry for the doctor if I knew everything. She thought that if I knew the doctor could go to jail, and I might lose my job if he left, I would be quiet," Emma said. Jessica wanted to roll her eyes at the ignorance of Sheila. She was glad of it, but it was stupid. "I think she also liked to gloat and feel important," Emma added. Jessica could only agree with that assessment.

"Anyway, after I figured everything out and saw the doctor's appointment book of when he was going to be at the clinic, I thought that was when the fake birth would happen. So, I told Felipe, and he told Christina what was going to happen. You know what happened next." Emma sat very quietly with her hands folded in her lap. Jessica put her hand over Emma's. Emma looked up at Jessica.

"They'll never find out from me," Jessica said. "I'm going to get this creep, and I'll see if I can't help you find a new job if you should lose this one when we send him to jail."

"I'm sorry I didn't tell sooner," Emma answered. Jessica shook her head.

"You have no reason to be sorry," Jessica replied. "I've got some other people to interview to get them to admit the truth now. Are you going to be ok?"

Emma nodded and stood up. Jessica stood up as well and hugged Emma. Jessica thanked her again and headed out the door to her partners. She was ready to take down this dirty doctor and whoever his money man was.

Jessica and the Williamses
Earlier at the Williamses' Home

Chapter 61

After Chet and Ron left, Jessica spun around to face the Williamses. They both looked physically ill. Jessica went and sat down in a chair and got comfortable. Mark and Carrie were sitting on the couch. Jessica looked over at them and smiled.

"Here's the deal," she began. "I'm going to bust everyone involved with the kidnapping of the baby." A look of relief started to make its way across the Williamses' faces. Jessica continued. "And, that includes you two." The look quickly vanished.

"Listen," Mark began. Jessica almost leapt forward in her chair and slammed her hand on the table.

"You had better understand that I have no use for lies at this moment," she said quietly, but forcefully. Her face was covered in fury. "So unless you're about to tell me the God's honest truth, you had just better sit there in silence. Are we clear?" The couple nodded, almost as one. Jessica straightened her jacket and leaned back in the chair.

"Now," she continued. "Where were we? Oh, yes. I am going to have everyone arrested that was involved in kidnapping of this baby. My only question is did you know that this child was the son of a vet who died overseas, and he and his wife had cleaned up part of the drug trade in this city?"

Horror covered both of the Williamses' faces. Jessica had suspected as much. Mark looked like he was dying to defend himself. Jessica smiled internally. This was almost too easy.

"You look like you want to speak, Mark," Jessica began. Mark nodded. "That's probably not a good idea."

139

Mark looked confused. "You're probably going to need a lawyer." Mark shook his head.

"Listen, I don't need a lawyer," Mark pleaded. "We thought we were adopting a baby. The doctor told us something went wrong, and it would take months or even a year to straighten everything out now that the other lady lost the baby. The doctor assured us the best thing to do was to fake a delivery." Carrie was near tears. Jessica had no sympathy for her at all.

"Didn't that seem the least bit, oh, I don't know, ILLEGAL?" Jessica spat out. Carrie burst into tears, and Mark was looking at Jessica helplessly while trying to comfort his wife.

"The doctor told us we were saving the baby," he explained. Jessica really wanted to slap some sense into the man but resisted. "He told us about how the baby was going to be brought up in a drug infested neighborhood and probably wouldn't live to see his fifteenth birthday." Jessica rubbed her hand against her temple. She hated to admit it, but these two weren't any masterminds. Their biggest crime was being stupid. "We'll testify against the doctor," Mark added, trying to get out of the mess he finally realized he and his wife were in.

"I've got enough to get the doctor," Jessica said. That wasn't really true, but she wasn't about to show them that she could use them. Right now, she had the leverage, and she wanted to keep it that way.

"What if we testify against the lawyer and the money guy, Arachnid?" Mark asked. Jessica couldn't help herself as her head popped up. Maybe she could use these two.

Chapter 62

"Are you sure about that name?" Jessica asked, trying to appear as disinterested as possible. Mark looked at Carrie for help. She was too busy crying. She shook her head.

"I think it was something like Paperclip, or Glue, or some other office product. That was the last name," she said through sobs. Jessica wanted to strangle both of them. Mark snapped his fingers.

"Staples!" he exclaimed. Jessica wanted to do a touchdown celebration dance.

"Arachnid Staples?" she asked. Mark shook his head.

"That's not quite right," he said. "We never talked to him or saw him. I just heard the doctor mention him." Jessica wanted to groan.

"Archibald?" Mark asked, turning to his wife. Jessica did her best not to let her body tense or give any indication that was the correct name. Carrie thought for a second and nodded her head slowly. "Archibald Staples," Mark said, hesitantly to Jessica.

"You're sure?" Jessica asked. She was sitting in the chair, with her legs crossed and her left hand covering her mouth. Her left elbow was propped up on the arm of the chair. It took everything in her to act nonchalantly. Mark looked at Carrie who nodded. Mark nodded. Jessica uncrossed her legs and leaned forward.

"You two will testify against the doctor, lawyer, and this Archibald guy if necessary?" she asked. They both nodded. "Well, I can't promise anything, but I think we might be able to get reduced or no jail time."

Carrie burst into tears, and Mark looked distraught. Jessica silently knew that these two would never last one day in jail. She got up, walked into the kitchen, pulled out her cellphone, and made a call. The phone rang a couple of times on the other end, and Trip answered.

141

"What do you have, Agent?" Trip asked.

"A mess, sir," Jessica replied. "I'm not saying I have, but if I would have stumbled upon a baby buying case, how interested are we in prosecuting a couple whose biggest mistake seems to be being stupid?" Trip chuckled.

"What are we talking about, Jessica?" he asked.

"I have a couple who said they would testify about everyone involved," Jessica replied. "They were told the child was given up for adoption. The mother, who the doctor assumed had substance abuse problems, was told the child died. They aren't the ringleaders. They're just rich and very stupid."

"They'll give us bigger fish?" Trip asked. Jessica smiled. If you only knew, sir, she thought.

"Yeah, much bigger names," she replied vaguely.

"I think we can let them go with some probation or something like that. No jail time," Trip responded.

"They wouldn't last a day in jail, sir," Jessica responded. "I'll get them to talk. Thanks, Trip."

"Any time, Jessica," Trip replied and disconnected. Jessica walked back into the living room and decided it was time to let the Williamses off the hook.

Chapter 63

Jessica walked into the room and observed the Williamses. They were holding each other. Mark was trying to comfort Carrie. Jessica sighed. These two weren't bad people; they had just made some dumb decisions. Sam had always told Jessica that people would do dumb things when it came to their kids or to have kids. Jessica didn't know their back story. Maybe they couldn't have children. She wasn't excusing what they did; in fact, there was a part of it that was noble, incredibly stupid, but noble. They were trying to help a child that they thought was going to have a very rough life. She cleared her throat, and the couple turned to see she had entered the room.

Jessica walked back over to the chair she had been sitting in earlier and sat back down.

"How did you pay for the baby?" she asked.

"When the lawyer was removed from the equation after the first baby died, I had to have some money transferred to a Swiss bank account," Mark replied. Jessica nodded. That had to be Sheila Long's account. The poor fool, she thought. They've made her look like the person in charge of the money. Jessica was really going to enjoy seeing her squirm in the box when she got her. She tore herself away from her thoughts and turned back to the Williamses.

"Would you be willing to testify to that as well?" Jessica asked. Mark nodded. "If you're willing to testify to everything you've said, I don't think either of you will do any jail time." The two of them looked relieved with that information.

"You two need to realize the second chance you're getting," Jessica said, looking first at Mark and then at Carrie. They both nodded. Jessica sighed and decided she had scolded them enough. She reached into her pocket and pulled out her card and gave one to both of them.

"Here's the deal," she began. "You don't leave the area, you don't tell anyone what happened, you don't speak to the doctor, or the nurse, or anyone else involved with this case. Are we clear?" Both of the Williamses nodded that they understood. Jessica stood up. "Don't do anything as stupid as this again," she added. The Williamses hastily agreed. Jessica walked over to the door and looked back at them. The couple was hugging each other, in relief. Jessica nodded, telling herself this was the right thing to do and opened the door.

Jessica walked outside. She was formulating a plan of how to bring down the good doctor and his nurse. As she stepped outside and joined her two partners, she thought she could never blame John again for the production he made each time he solved a case.

Jessica and Sheila, Earlier, FBI Field Office Miami, Florida

Chapter 64

Jessica walked into the interview room. Ron and Chet were out looking for the track suit Jessica had requested. A camera was running in the observation room to record everything. Jessica tossed a file down on the table and sat down in the chair across from Sheila. She leaned back in the chair with her arms crossed. She looked at Sheila and just shook her head.

"Perhaps we got off on the wrong foot earlier," Sheila began. Jessica was having none of it. She uncrossed her arms, leaned forward, and put both hands on the table, palms down.

"Or, maybe you just made a mistake by not telling me the whole truth," Jessica countered. Sheila held her hands up, and began to shake her head. She was trying to figure out what to say. Jessica didn't give her a chance. She pounced like a lion stalking an injured animal.

"Perhaps I gave you a chance earlier to tell me everything, and you flat blew it," Jessica said, standing.

"Where are you going?" Sheila asked. Jessica shrugged.

"Wherever I want," she responded. "You've done nothing but tell me half-truths. I don't need you; I just wanted to show you how serious I was earlier today about dragging you down here. You're going to jail for a very long time, and the sad fact is all you had to do was tell me the truth, and maybe we could have avoided that." Jessica started around the table toward the door.

"You can't do that," Sheila snapped. Jessica turned quickly. She crossed the space between them in three strides. She had her right hand on the back of Sheila's

145

chair and her left on the table in front of her. She leaned in to where her face was inches from Sheila's. Jessica could smell the fear in Sheila; Jessica got a grin on her face. If Sheila didn't know better, she would have thought that Jessica was enjoying this.

"What's wrong?" Jessica asked softly. "Don't like it when someone shows you how little power you have and you're at someone else's mercy?"

Sheila swallowed and tried to collect herself. Jessica pressed on.

"You are nothing but the idiot that got caught with the Swiss bank account," Jessica continued. "It's going to look like you're the money man, not the doctor, but then again, that's none of my business."

"I don't know what you're talking about," Sheila said, trying to set up straight and appear indignant.

"I'm talking about the money that went into your account when the baby was kidnapped, the account that's none of my business," Jessica replied quietly with a broad smile on her face. "Exactly how long do you think you're going to last in gen pop when the other inmates find out you were responsible for kidnapping a child and selling it?" Horror struck Sheila's eyes. Jessica felt a little satisfied inside. After what Sheila had done to Emma, Jessica thought that the fear Sheila was feeling was just the beginning.

Chapter 65

"I, I didn't do that," Sheila stuttered. Jessica stood over her mock nodding like she understood.

"I'm sure you didn't," Jessica answered. "But, the evidence shows that's exactly what you did. You're too dumb to be the mastermind of this scam." Jessica knew she was being a little harsh, but at right this second, she could care less.

"You don't understand," Sheila began. Jessica lifted her hands off the table and chair and shrugged.

"You're right," she replied. "Remember, it's none of my business." With that, Jessica turned, walked over to the door, grabbed the handle, opened the door, and walked out. Behind her, Sheila was screaming for her to wait. Jessica ignored her and walked down the hall. She heard the door click and rushed into the observation room. Sheila was sobbing. She was absolutely beside herself. Jessica watched, enjoying the show. Jessica set a timer on her watch for fifteen minutes, sat down, and began to check her email on one of the computers in the room. She propped her feet up and got comfortable. Every once in a while, a wail from the integration room would get her attention, but for the most part, she tuned it out. Her alarm went off, and she looked in on the nurse. Sheila looked distraught, but more importantly, broken.

"Showtime," Jessica said, a little too happily. She took her feet off the table, headed out of the observation room, and stopped in front of the interrogation room. Jessica made sure she was prepared, put her most irritated face on, and slammed the door against the wall as she opened it. Sheila nearly fell out of her chair; Jessica had scared her so badly. Jessica looked at Sheila with undisguised contempt on her face. Jessica slammed a notepad on the table and went over to her chair but didn't sit down. She looked at Sheila and just shook her head in disgust. Jessica crossed her arms and stood with one foot

147

slightly in front of the other, looking down on Sheila. Sheila looked up at Jessica, tears in her eyes, her spirit completely broken.

"Today's your lucky day," Jessica said. "They want the big fish. They don't want you. They want you to testify. I don't agree with them. I think you're the worst of the bunch. You didn't do this for money; you didn't do this for any reason, but because you held power over innocent people. You took away a child from a mother that you knew was okay. You tried to destroy a family just because you wanted to have a power trip." Jessica thought about the words she was saying right now and realized that someone could accuse her of the same thing. The difference was Jessica was telling the truth. No one wanted the little peon nurses; they wanted the big fish in this ring. Jessica knew she had to completely break Sheila to get what she needed to put away Archibald. During her pause, Sheila finally spoke.

"I'll give you everything. Just please don't put me in jail; they'll kill me," she pleaded. Jessica uncrossed her arms and leaned forward, her palms resting on the table. She lowered her face down until she was just inches away from Sheila.

"You tell me even one lie," Jessica began. "I'll have them throw you in the gen pop and let everyone know that you kidnapped a baby. Heck, I might even suggest that you abused the child before you sold it. Are we clear?" Sheila was nodding, tears streaming down her face. Jessica straightened, nodded, and sat down in the chair. "Tell me everything."

Chapter 66

"It all began when that prostitute lost the baby," Sheila said quietly. It was apparent she had accepted her fate. "Brian owed a lot of money to a bookie, and he was going to use the money from the adoption, which was legal, to pay for it. Apparently, he figured out how much he was going to have left over and thought he knew a sure thing in some game. I couldn't tell you what sport it was. He was just raving for days about how he was about to get completely out of debt. The thing was, if the fool would just have paid off what he owed and quit gambling what he thought was his future winnings, he wouldn't have been in this mess."

Sheila paused for a second, and Jessica thought how glad she was Chet wasn't here right now. He had been beating himself up for several days, but to hear this story would probably remind him of the mess he had found himself in. Jessica pulled herself out of her thoughts as Sheila began to continue her story.

"I knew the doctor was in bad shape, so I suggested that he just use another girl," Sheila said. She looked at Jessica hopelessly. "You have to understand; all I did was see the girl's address. I just assumed she was like all the others, either a prostitute, or a drug user, or who knows what. I never thought she was an upstanding citizen."

"It never occurred to you that a mother deserves to raise her child?" Jessica asked. Sheila gave Jessica a withered look.

"How many times do we have to tell you?" Sheila asked. "Don't you get it? Most of these moms don't want the kid. We thought we were doing her a favor."

Jessica shook her head. She never thought that any child should be brought up in an environment like Sheila was describing, but at the same time, who had made her and the doctor judge, jury, and executioner when it came to these mothers?

"Anyway," Sheila continued. "She had the baby, and I took it out of the room. We used a few drugs to leave her confused and disoriented and then told her the baby was dead. We then asked if she would like us to take care of the arrangements. We had given her a little something to make her susceptible to suggestions. The lady agreed, and I thought everything was fine. Boy, was I wrong."

Sheila sat there, looking at the wall blankly.

"And the bank account?" Jessica asked. Sheila waved her hand.

"The bank account was put in my name so if anyone ever thought something of the doctor and started looking, they couldn't find anything directly tying him to what had happened," Sheila replied.

"Didn't it ever occur to you that someone might check you out since you work directly with him?" Jessica asked. A thoughtful look came over Sheila's face. She shook her head.

"No," she replied. "I can honestly say it never occurred to either of us that someone might check my bank accounts."

Jessica felt like slapping her forehead with her hand. She had what she needed. She went to the door and left. She went down the hall and found one of the guards. She had the guard take Sheila back to lockup. As she watched Sheila be taken away, Chet and Ron showed up with the track suit. It was time for Jessica's big finale.

Now, FBI Field Office
Miami, Florida

Chapter 67
In the interrogation room, Ron turned to Chet. Chet had a smile that threatened to crack his face in half.

"Did you know?" Ron asked, shocked. Chet smiled and shrugged.

"I was beginning to suspect," Chet admitted. "I wasn't for sure, but when Jessica began the interrogation by showing a track suit of Carrie's and then said only DNA, it began to click. She never said it, but all she had to do was check the child's DNA against the parents, and it was over. But, more importantly, the doctor knew it." Chet turned and looked back in the observation room where Trip was trying to wrap his head around what was going on. The attorney for the Department of Justice was on the phone, getting more excited by the minute.

"What about Christina Lopez and the child?" Ron asked. Chet turned toward Ron, somber.

"I don't know," Chet replied. "We have to let them know that we know the truth, but we can't put it on the news until we bring down Archibald. There's no reason for her to be hiding out, but I don't know how to let her know." Ron stood for a second thinking. He began to leave the room.

"Let me take care of it," Ron said, exiting the room. Chet watched him leave and then turned his attention back to the interrogation room. Trip was leaning in toward Jessica.

"Let me make absolutely sure I have this right," Trip said, voice low. "This guy faked a baby's death, was going to sell it to the couple that was in the clinic, but before that could happen, the real mother stormed the clinic with some unknown accomplices, and took the baby back?"

"The accomplices may not be so unknown," Jessica admitted. "But, yes, for the most part, that's it."

"Then, why did the doctor call the police?" Trip asked. Jessica smiled.

"He didn't," Jessica responded. "The group tripped a silent alarm. Now, I'm sure the doctor could have fixed that problem, but a nurse at the clinic arrived while the still hysterical, soon-to-be mother by way of purchase, was crying uncontrollably. Trip, it was simply a matter of bad timing." Trip leaned back, shaking his head and chuckling. He looked Jessica right in the eye.

"You know, you never would have pulled a stunt like that before," Trip said. Jessica smiled and tried to look a little ashamed, but failed.

"I know; he's rubbing off on me," she admitted quietly. Trip shook his head.

"No, Jessica," Trip began, quietly but strongly. "You've got your confidence back. You are one great agent with or without John Fowler. This one is all your win, and you should celebrate it." Jessica nearly blushed from the compliment, but inside she was doing a fist pump and shouting, "Yes!"

Chapter 68

Ron had been thinking how to handle things as he drove to Christina's apartment complex. When he pulled up, he saw the group of men he had been told about by Jessica. Ron got out of the car and walked over to the group sitting and standing by the front steps. The group was positioned where people could easily walk up and down the steps, but they could block them if they needed to. They seemed to tense up as he approached and started to cover the steps until one of them gave a sign for them to wait.

"Something wrong?" the young man who seemed to be the leader of the gang asked.

"Are you Felipe?" Ron asked. Felipe looked a little surprised but nodded. "I'm Ronald McGuire, FBI." As he told Felipe that, he showed all of them his badge. The group seemed to not be quite as intense after that. Ron pointed to an empty spot on the steps. Felipe nodded, and Ron sat down. He looked around for a second and then turned to face Felipe. "I wanted to ask you about Christina's husband, Oscar. Did you tell the FBI agent that was here earlier that he died overseas?" Felipe nodded. Ron nodded back and looked around again. He couldn't see any drug pushers anywhere. Ron had to admit; these young men had done what they set out to do. He turned back to Felipe.

"I served over there as well," Ron said. Felipe looked a little surprised. "I can't tell you exactly where. It's classified, but I understand what he went through. You've got to respect people like the Lopezes. All they wanted was to clean up this area and let people live peaceful lives. That's something to be proud of. You know what else is something to be proud of? Agreeing to be a part of the Lopezes' mission and going through with it was the right thing. Do you understand what I'm saying?" Felipe nodded. As he did so, he fiddled with something in his pocket. Ron noticed and continued.

"I'm not saying you have any way of contacting Christina, or that you know where she is, but if you did, I wish you'd tell her something for me." As Ron talked, he was watching each man's face. They gave away nothing. Ron paused, pursed his lips, and blew out his cheeks, trying to decide how to continue. "Tell her who I am. Tell her I am Ronald McGuire. I'm a former member of Delta Force and currently a member of the FBI. I don't tell many people about being Delta Force, but I need you to believe me, so I figured I have to give you something." Ron paused and continued quietly. "We figured it all out." Ron watched the men's faces. Some of them looked at each other, skeptically. Ron continued. "We know that she led a group of young men into the clinic not to kidnap a baby, but to bring it home."

Ron paused and watched them. Their faces gave away nothing. One young man glanced over Ron's shoulder at a building across the street. Ron didn't follow the gaze, but he felt he knew what the young man was looking at.

"Tell her that we have arrested the doctor, and we are going to take care of everything. Tell her I'm sorry for all she's been through. Tell her that we're sorry that she had to take care of this situation instead of the FBI. But, most importantly, tell her that if she ever needs anything, she can contact me at the FBI." Ron paused and looked down at the ground. He looked back up and smiled at Felipe. "You guys did good. You should be proud of yourselves, and I don't know if they ever told you, but I bet Christina and Oscar were proud of you too." Ron stood and reached his hand out to shake Felipe's hand. Felipe stood up and shook his hand. Ron moved to the next young man, and he did the same. Ron shook all their hands and began to walk back to the car. As he was walking he looked over to the spot at which one of the men had been looking over Ron's shoulder. There stood a lady holding what appeared to be a baby. Ron looked back at Felipe and tilted his head toward the lady. Felipe looked over at the lady for permission. She nodded, and Felipe nodded to Ron. Ron turned and walked over to meet Christina.

Chapter 69

Ron walked toward the lady he was sure was Christina Lopez.

"What did he do? Have a number pre-programmed on his phone?" Ron asked. The lady looked a little surprised that Ron had figured out how she had heard what was going on. As he got closer, he could see what looked like a Bluetooth ear piece in her ear.

"I've got to assume that you're Ronald McGuire, former Delta Force member, and now part of the FBI?" she asked, smiling. Ron returned the smile.

"Guilty as charged," Ron replied. "I have to assume that you are Christina Lopez?" Christina nodded. Ron moved closer to the baby. He ran a finger gently along the child's cheek and spoke very softly. "And, I have to assume that you're the little one that this whole case has been about?"

"His name is Oscar Jr.," Christina replied. Ron nodded in appreciation.

"You've got a great mom, little guy," Ron said softly. "You've also got a great dad to live up to." Ron noticed Christina tearing up as he talked. "You've already been a big help," he continued. "Because of you, we're about to bring down an illegal baby ring. That's some pretty good work to be less than a month old." Christina looked down at her baby proudly. Ron watched Christina with her son.

"I'm sorry, Christina," Ron said quietly. She looked at him and shook her head.

"There's nothing to be sorry about. I got my baby back, and those people are going to jail. What else is there?" she asked.

"You deserved better than that," Ron replied. He swept his arm out at the area. "Look around. You and your husband cleaned up this area. You made things better for everyone, and you got repaid by losing your husband

and a man kidnapping your child; that's not right."
Christina smiled at Ron and shook her head.

"What am I supposed to do, be mad?" she asked.
"No, we knew what we were getting into when we began to
clean up this neighborhood. Let's be honest. My husband
and I were lucky we didn't catch a bullet then." Ron had to
agree. Christina continued. "Have you ever wondered why
I went to all these lengths? It was for little Oscar here. His
father and I didn't want to raise our child in the community
the way it was. Do you know how you change that? You
work. You work to change things, and you don't stop until
it's done. This is my neighborhood, and my friends and I
are going to make it a safe place for Oscar to grow up.
Maybe one day, we'll see people everywhere fighting to
make a difference." Ron shook his head.

"Lady, you're brave," he replied. Christina shook
her head.

"No, Ron," she responded. "We were afraid for our
children's future. Sure, it was an unborn child, but it was
still my child. Do you know what a parent will do for a
child?" Ron shook his head.

"I don't have any children," Ron replied. "But, I do
know what I'd do for my parents. I know it's not the same,
but I'd move heaven and earth for them." Christina smiled
at Ron understandingly.

"Then you understand what I'll do for little Oscar?"
she asked. Ron nodded. He turned toward his car.

"Good luck to both of you," Ron said. "If you ever
need anything, please don't hesitate to contact me."

"Are you stationed in Miami permanently?" she
asked. Ron shrugged.

"I would like to be elsewhere, but I'm here for
now," he replied.

"You seem like the kind of man who gets what he
wants," Christina replied. Ron chuckled as he started
toward his car.

"I hope you're right," he called back. Ron got in his car and headed back to join the others. As he watched them disappear in his rearview mirror, he hoped Christina was right.

FBI Field Office
Miami, Florida

Chapter 70

Jessica waited for everyone to calm back down before she started back in on Dr. Nichols. She started to question the suspect when the attorney asked both Trip and Jessica to step outside.

"I need you two to listen to me very carefully," the attorney said. "That man in there is about to give us Archibald Staples. Do you understand what that means?" Jessica looked at the attorney like he had two heads. Trip closed his eyes and ran his hand over his head. Trip had been afraid of this. He opened his eyes and looked directly at the attorney.

"Let me handle this, okay?" he asked the attorney. The attorney nodded.

"Let's walk," Trip said to Jessica.

"What's going on, Trip?" Jessica asked.

"I am so glad John's not here," Trip said quietly. Thoughts ran through Jessica's mind. She stopped walking and turned toward Trip.

"This just got political, didn't it?" Jessica asked. Trip took her elbow and continued to lead her down the hall. He found another empty interrogation room and went inside with her.

"Listen," Trip began, but Jessica cut him off.

"This has to do with his son, doesn't it?!" Jessica demanded. Trip nodded. Jessica sighed, folded her arms, and looked away from Trip. She was trying not to explode on him, but that was proving difficult. "He's going to get off because his son was the former President of the United States!"

"That's right, Jessica," Trip said in stern voice. Jessica was taken aback. "I know exactly what you're thinking, but let me tell you something. His son was one of the most popular presidents of all time. His popularity ratings were through the roof. This is going to be painted as a picture of a man thinking that a child was going to be raised in the type of home that no child should be raised in. It's going to be painted that Brian made a mistake. One day, Kenneth Nichols will probably run for president again, and if I had any guess, he will win. I understand that you're not happy, but this is one of those times that I have to look at the big picture, whether I want to or not. We got a win." Jessica just stared daggers at Trip.

"Just a few weeks ago, you told John how you envied him for not having to deal with the politics of this job," she replied. Trip ran his hand over his head.

"Jessica, this is the way it's going to be," Trip replied, frustrated. "I'm sorry if that's not good enough for you. Now, I'm going in there to wrap this up. It's your case, and I would love for you to finish it off. However, if you can't control your temper or what you say to Dr. Nichols, I'm going to have to insist you sit this one out." Jessica shrugged.

"I guess you just benched me then, Coach!" she said. Jessica turned and marched back down the hall to the observation room where Chet was. In case there was any doubt in Trip's mind that Jessica was upset, that was erased when Trip jumped a little from the slamming door.

"There are days I hate this job," Trip said out loud to no one.

Chapter 71

Jessica stood in the observation room just seething. Chet had nearly jumped through the ceiling when she slammed the door. He stood there for a second, trying to figure out if he should talk to her or not. She turned toward him, taking the decision out of his hands.

"They are only going to ask him about this case, Chet," she said, anger still radiating off her. "They're only interested in getting Archibald on this one charge."

Chet stood there, trying to put it all together. He assumed it all had to do with Dr. Brian Nichols' son, the former president.

"Kenneth is going to run for president again, and no one wants to drag his name through any more mud than necessary," she said, answering Chet's unspoken question. Chet knew that Jessica had questions in the deaths of the other infants that Dr. Nichols was involved in.

"What about the other kids!?" Jessica blurted out, still obviously frustrated. "How do we know they weren't sold on the black market or that Archibald wasn't involved? Huh?" She crossed her arms and began to tap her foot. Chet really wasn't sure what to do at this point.

"I guess it doesn't really matter now, does it?" she asked. Chet had no idea what to say.

"Thanks for listening, Chet," she said, appreciation on her face. Chet smiled and nodded, not sure what he had actually done. There was a knock on the door, and then it opened. Ron stuck his head in.

"Can I come in?" he asked. Jessica nodded. "I've talked to Christina," he said. Jessica looked impressed.

"How did you find her?" she asked.

"The group that hangs out on the steps of her apartment building knew where she was. They passed the message for me. She and the baby are okay. She named him after her husband, Oscar," he replied.

"That's pretty good work," Chet said. Ron shrugged.

"Jessica did all the heavy lifting," Ron replied. "Once we knew that she was the real mother, everything just kind of fit into place."

"Like a jigsaw puzzle," Jessica said, casting a quick glance at Chet. Chet chuckled.

"John always said every mystery works itself out into a perfect picture; you just have to know how to read the picture," Chet said. Jessica shook her head.

"Looks like it's action time," Ron said, pointing at the interview room. Jessica and Chet turned and watched Trip come back in.

Chapter 72

After taking a minute to calm down after his and Jessica's little tiff in the hall, Trip straightened his coat, checked his tie, and walked down the hall. He reached the interrogation room, opened the door, stepped inside, and shut it behind him. The attorney looked a little confused when Jessica didn't come in with him.

"It's just going to be us," Trip told the attorney who still was a little confused. Trip took his place and turned toward Dr. Nichols. "So, tell me what happened," Trip said. Brian folded his hands together and began.

"I have spent my entire life trying to bring children into this world. Too many times I've seen children come along that their parents didn't want. Or, worse than that, they think that the child is going to be the end of their life, the end of their fun, the end of their being able to be themselves. Nothing makes me more ill than to see these children that the parents don't want and then to work with all these parents who would give anything to have a child, parents who would give the child every advantage in the world. People will pay tens or hundreds of thousands of dollars just to have a child. People who have money to literally burn want to raise children and can't. What have I done that's so terrible? Tell me that. What have I done?"

"We're not here to debate the state of the world or whether something is right or wrong, Dr. Nichols. We're here for you to tell us what happened in this kidnapping case," the attorney said to the doctor. Brian nodded.

"Let me remind you, Doctor. The lady you stole the baby from wanted that child, and you took it from her. That's called kidnapping every day of the week," Trip responded to the doctor's question.

"That's what I'm saying," the doctor countered. "I wouldn't have been put in that spot if it wasn't for the rules that are in place. See, when that girl lost her baby after her pimp hit her, I didn't have anywhere else to turn."

"You are sitting here trying to blame someone else for this mess?!?" Trip asked, shocked at the gall of the doctor.

"Enough!" the lawyer shouted. "We aren't here to argue. I want to know what happened, and that's it." Trip was trying to calm himself down. He had turned a few shades of red during the doctor's last speech. The doctor continued.

"The prostitute who lost the baby had signed over the baby," the doctor said. Trip was shaking his head disgustedly. "Anyway, it was all legal." Trip looked at the doctor skeptically. "You can question the morals of it, or if it worked its way faster through the system than most, but it was all legal. Once the child died though, I was left scrambling."

"Why didn't you just give back the money you were fronted after the baby died?" Trip asked.

"You're jumping ahead of the story, but the short answer is I owed money to a bookie," Brian replied. Trip brightened at that answer.

"You don't say?" Trip asked smiling. "What's your bookie's name, Brian? You say the right name, and you'll just make my day."

Chapter 73

"I need to see you outside," the lawyer said to Trip. Trip held his hand up, looking at Brian with anticipation for the name he was about to give.

"As soon as he tells me the bookie," Trip answered, still staring at Brian.

"No, now," the attorney replied. Trip turned toward the lawyer. Disgust started to cover his face. "Outside, Mr. Smothers," the lawyer said. Trip got up and threw his chair as he did. He was almost to the door when he stopped, wheeled, and slammed both hands on the table, causing the lawyer to jump back and Dr. Nichols to about fall out of his chair.

"You tell them," Trip began, his voice low but deadly threatening. "You tell those scumbags, whoever they are, and wherever they are; I'm going to turn over every rock in every square inch of this country until I find them. And then, I'm going to throw them in the darkest, deepest hole that exists, and they are never, EVER getting out. You make sure they know that."

The attorney had recovered and was trying to push Trip, but Trip wouldn't move. He cut the attorney a sideways glance, and he backed up. Trip stood up, straightened his tie, and turned towards the lawyer.

"You keep your filthy hands off me," he said and then turned and exited the room. The attorney followed right behind him. The attorney slammed the door and began to dress down Trip. Down the hall where neither man could see, the observation room door cracked open, and three sets of eyes peered out.

"What do you think you're doing in there?" the lawyer demanded of Trip. Trip ignored him, and kept his back to him. "I'm talking to you," the lawyer said and grabbed Trip by the left shoulder and spun him around. As Trip spun, he cocked his right hand and punched the lawyer right on the jaw, dropping him to the ground. The three onlookers in the observation room all jumped, but none of them ran out.

"I told you not to touch me," Trip said, standing over the downed lawyer.

"Are you crazy?" the lawyer asked. Trip squatted down beside him.

"You tell Archibald and whoever else is in on this thing that 'By the Book Lionel' has left the FBI. The man in charge of the New York division of the FBI is going to devote every remaining resource I have available to catching them!"

The lawyer glared at Trip. And then, he slowly began to smile. He checked his lip with the back of his hand as he chuckled.

"You think you're smart, don't you?" the lawyer asked as Trip remained squatted beside him, nodding his head. "You don't have a clue who they are, and you're not going to. That's the beauty of it, you fool. Archibald was always set up as the lightning rod to take all the heat. You can dig all you want, but no one is going to tell you what you want to know." Trip leaned in very close.

"And, here's what you don't know," Trip said in a low voice. "I have someone that knows more than you'd believe. We're just getting started. Look at how easily we brought down this part of your enterprise. Just wait until we get a little bit of time and figure it all out. You tell your bosses that they haven't got a chance. And, when you call Duck later, make sure and give him a good quack from me. Do your job; get the evidence on Archibald. Feel free to tell your superiors in the US Attorney's office what I did to you, and feel free to tell your real superiors what I did to you and what I said. You see, here's the thing. We know Sam was killed because of them. I know Sam died because I did nothing, and now, I have nothing left to lose."

Trip stood up. James reached up for help, and Trip scoffed at him. Trip turned and went down to the

166

observation room. As he opened the door, he heard scrambling. He smiled. He had forgotten they were in there when he slugged the attorney. He looked back at James picking himself up off the floor. Trip opened the door and went inside. The three agents were all trying to act like nothing happened. Trip shook his head. He looked over at Jessica who cracked a smile.

"Nice shot, Boss," she said. "You should have put him in an armbar and broke his arm." Trip began to laugh.

"Well, I guess I'm in trouble," Trip said. "He's got three witnesses."

"You see anything?" Jessica asked Ron. Ron shook his head. Jessica turned to Chet. "You see anything?" Jessica asked Chet. Chet shook his head. Jessica turned back to Trip, smiling. "I'm not sure what you're talking about, Boss. We've been observing the prisoner while you two, we can only assume, were discussing interrogation strategy. "

Trip smiled at Jessica.

"You were right; I was wrong. That guy is a rat," Trip said.

"Now, if only I could teach John that," Jessica said. Ron looked confused, and Jessica quickly added, "Which of course is impossible now that he is dead." The room was quiet with an uncomfortable silence.

Chapter 74

The door opened in the interrogation room and the four watched the attorney walk back into the room.

"Aren't you worried that he's going to mess this up, Boss?" Chet asked. Trip turned toward Chet, shaking his head.

"Nope," Trip replied. "Archibald has been set up as the fall guy, and they don't want to lose their rat in the US Attorney's office. He's a snake, but he's going to do what is best for them and today, what's best for them just happens to line up with what's best for us. I just wish I could have gotten Brian to admit that Duck was his bookie. That would have gone a long way to tying Duck and Archibald together." Trip smiled at Chet. "We might have been able to bring down your cabal with that information, Chet." Chet smiled.

The attorney took his seat and began his interrogation of the doctor.

"Director Smothers won't be joining us," the attorney began. "He has some other business to take care of. Now, will you please tell me what happened? The baby you were going to have adopted by the Williamses died, and your financial backer wanted his money back. Is that correct?"

"Yes," Brian answered.

"Who was your financial backer?" the attorney asked.

"Archibald Staples," Brian answered. In the observation room, Jessica did a fist pump, and Trip clapped his hands together.

"Game, set, and match," Trip muttered. Chet and Jessica gave each other a high five. In the interrogation room, Brian continued.

"I told Archibald what happened, and he told me he didn't care," Brian explained. "I told him the only way that we were going to be able to get the funds he required would be to sell a baby. He told me that was fine by him. So, we set up the bank account in Sheila Long's name and sold the child the Williamses received. We convinced them that they would be doing the child a favor, which I really thought we would." The attorney gave the doctor a look for getting off track again. The doctor sighed and continued.

"Anyway, we told Christina that her baby was dead and convinced her to let us take care of the arrangements. Sheila hid the baby in the hospital, and we bribed a guard to not notice anything to get the baby out of the hospital. I made the exchange with the Williamses at the clinic. I don't know how Christina figured everything out."

"Has Archibald been paid?" the attorney asked.

"Yes," Brian responded. "As soon as the Williamses paid Sheila, she transferred the money Archibald was owed."

The attorney dug through his notes and found the bank account. The attorney knew the account had already been drained of the funds, but that was privileged information.

"Everything looks good here," the attorney answered. "I'll check with everyone else, but I think it's time you go with the US Marshals. We'll get more in depth closer to the time of the trial, but I have what I need to get started. I've got to go make some calls to prepare a warrant for Archibald Staples." With that, the attorney left the room. He walked over to the observation room and went inside.

"Can I trust you not to bother him while I get your warrant?" the attorney seemed to sneer at Trip.

"You have my word I won't talk to him," Trip answered. The attorney nodded and left.

"I didn't agree to any of those terms," Jessica said to Trip. Trip looked at Jessica and rubbed his head with his hand.

"And I always thought John was the troublemaker of the group," Trip answered.

"Who do you think he learned it from?" Jessica asked.

Chapter 75

"Can you please just give me five minutes with him?" Jessica asked. "For John?" Trip didn't look happy about the idea, but relented and nodded.

"I've got some phone calls to make to prepare the team," he replied. "I'll make sure no one bothers you."

Jessica entered the interrogation room. Dr. Nichols was still sitting there, looking exhausted. Jessica went and sat down in front of him.

"Listen," she began. "There's something I absolutely need to know." Brian waved her off.

"I've got nothing else to say to you," he responded. "I've told them everything I told them I would. If the US Attorney's office has something else to ask me, then I will gladly talk to them, but I have nothing to say to you."

Jessica stared at the doctor for a minute, trying to figure out how to get him to change his mind. She decided to go for broke.

"Sam Moore," she simply said. The doctor's head snapped up. Jessica knew she had him just for a second, so she pounced.

"I don't know who the father was of that baby, and frankly, I don't care," Jessica began. "All I want to know is did that baby survive? You have full immunity. Her widower just died, and Arthur and Madeline have no one left. Please, I need to know. Is Sam's baby alive?"

Brian just stared at Jessica. Jessica really wished John was here right now. She could get nothing off Brian. All the tricks John had tried to show her had come up empty. Jessica was starting to feel helpless.

"Sam's baby died," Brian replied quietly. "I'm sorry." Brian lowered his head. Jessica started to ask more when the door burst open, and the lawyer came into the room followed by Trip.

"What do you think you're doing?" he demanded. Trip gave her an apologetic look. Jessica gave the attorney a sad smile.

"I was asking him about an old friend of mine," Jessica replied. "That's all." With that, she got up and left the room. The attorney looked like he wanted to yell but didn't know what to yell about. Trip patted the attorney on the shoulder and told him he'd take care of it. Trip left the room, leaving Brain and the attorney by themselves. Trip caught up to Jessica in the hall. She had one arm pressed up against the wall with her head resting on her arm.

Trip came up to her and put his hand on her shoulder.

"Are you okay?" he asked. Jessica turned toward him with tears in her eyes.

"Brian said the baby was dead. John was so sure," she answered. Trip nodded.

"He doesn't get everything right," Trip replied. Jessica straightened up and nodded. She had a hurt look on her face.

"But, he's usually not wrong on something like this," she replied. With that, she turned and walked away. Trip's cellphone rang at that moment, so he had to let her go. As he went to answer the phone, Trip wondered if John and Jessica would ever get total closure.

Jessica continued up the hallway. Ron and Chet ran into her. She shook her head when they started to ask what was wrong. The three silently went to a waiting vehicle. They were headed to Archibald Staples's mansion to arrest him. Jessica always thought this would be a happier moment. She knew she had to tell John that Sam's baby was dead. She had no idea how he would react to that.

Chapter 76

"Look, I know that I can't have contact with the outside world, but may I talk to my son, the former president, before I go away?" Brian asked the attorney. The attorney looked irritated but agreed. "May I use my own phone?" Brian asked. The attorney didn't like it but agreed to it. Brian was left in private. His hands shook as he hit the preprogrammed button. The phone rang twice before it was answered on the other end.

"This is Kenneth," his son answered. Brain swallowed and gathered his courage.

"Son," Brain began. "I have done something wrong, and I need you to listen."

"Okay," Kenneth answered hoping his father remembered all of the pre-planned codes they had come up with if this day ever happened.

"I kidnapped a baby of someone I thought was an unfit mother and sold it to a well-off family," Brain said. Kenneth was pleased so far.

"Dad!" he exclaimed, hoping his shock sounded genuine enough in case someone was listening in.

"There's more," Brain said. "I had some financial backing on this, and the government wants me to turn state's evidence on him. I am going into protective custody, and you're not going to see me again."

"Okay, Dad," Kenneth said. "Are you going to prison?"

"No, Son," Brian answered. "I made this mistake. I thought I was doing what was best for the child, but I was wrong. All of these years of seeing these children treated wrong, and I just snapped. I want to assure you this has never happened before, and obviously, it's never going to happen again. The child has been reunited with its mother." Kenneth breathed an internal sigh of relief with that news.

Brian had just told Kenneth by their prearranged code that no one knew of any other incidents. He and Duck were safe. Archibald was in a little bit of trouble, but nothing they couldn't fix, and honestly, the authorities hardly knew anything. This could all be salvaged, and possibly, his father could be saved as well. Kenneth had no real affection for the man, but he was his father after all. Kenneth prepared himself for his big finale.

"Dad, I'm proud of you," Kenneth said. "You're doing the right thing. You did something wrong, and now, you're atoning for it. A son could never ask for a better role model. I'll see if I can't find a way to see you once everything is settled. You know I still have a little pull," he said, chuckling. Kenneth felt like he needed a drink after that lie.

"Thank you, Son," Brian answered. "If I don't see you, I'll understand."

"Don't worry, Dad," Kenneth replied with an evil smile on his face. "You'll see me sooner than you think." Kenneth disconnected.

Brian looked at the phone and turned it off. He believed his son, and he was afraid of what that last bit meant. There was nothing he could do. He had been warned by the three men he worked for what would happen to him if he ever got caught. He should have retired long ago, but he enjoyed the money too much. Brian would like to think that Archibald had driven Kenneth to new depths of evil, but Brian knew that wasn't true. While Archibald helped Kenneth cultivate his sick, twisted mind, Kenneth was the most evil creature Brain had ever had the misfortune of meeting. Brian thought he was living on borrowed time, and it may have just gotten shorter. For a brief second, he thought about telling the authorities everything, but then, he knew he wouldn't just die but be tortured as well. Brian sat down at the table in front of him and wept.

In the other room, the attorney's phone rang. Kenneth verified everything his father told him with the attorney and disconnected. Kenneth hoped he was able to let his father live, but if not, then that was part of business. Business he would personally take care of.

James walked back into the interrogation room and was surprised to see Trip standing there.

"James," Trip began smiling. "Did you think I was going to leave you alone with the witness until the US Marshals got here? Oh, you seem to have something on the edge of your lip there," Trip said, pointing to the small cut on the attorney's lip that Trip had cut earlier when he hit him. Trip smiled at the attorney. James looked very uncomfortable and sat down to wait for the Marshals to show up. Brian looked from one man to the other. What had he gotten himself into, he wondered.

John Fowler
Moore Residence

Chapter 77

John was covered in sweat. He had pushed himself
as far as he dared today with his physical therapy. The
doctor had told him he had to expect it to take some time
for him to recover, but John thought this was ridiculous.
He had been shot, not had his legs removed and then
reattached, but that was how it felt to him. John heard a
familiar song and realized it was his cellphone going off,
and if he had put the song on the phone correctly, that
meant Jessica was calling him. John found his phone and
saw it was her.

"Hello," he said, trying to disguise his voice.

"John?" Jessica asked. "Is that you?" Hearing
Jessica's voice, John relaxed.

"Yeah, it's me," John replied.

"Why the weird voice?" she asked.

"I wanted to make sure it was you," he replied.
"You never know who's listening in on these things."
There was silence on the other end. "Jess? You still
there?"

"John," Jessica began, somewhat flabbergasted but
knowing she shouldn't be. "You do realize if someone was
listening in, they would still be even though it's me on the
phone?" There was silence on John's end. Jessica laughed.
"John? John are you there?"

"I don't know if I should respond to that," John
replied. Jessica laughed even harder.

"It's okay, John. I had Chet sweep the phone for
bugs," Jessica said, knowing it was a lie. She was willing
to try anything to get John's mind off someone listening in
to the conversation.

"That was smart thinking," John replied. Jessica had to stifle a laugh. He paused for a second. "Who called who?"

"I called you," Jessica said, trying to steer the conversation back to the original point of the call. "John, I called to tell you that Doctor Nichols has implicated Archibald Staples. We have him, John. We're going to arrest him!"

"When and where?" John asked, the weariness leaving his body.

"Un-uh," Jessica said. "I need you to promise me that you're not going to be a part of the bust." John was silent. "Johnnn!" John was still silent. "Jonathan Edward Fowler!"

"My name's not Jonathan. It's just John," John replied.

"I know that," Jessica said, getting frustrated.

"I promise I won't be part of your team that busts him," John said.

"That was a little too easy," Jessica said.

"Is that bad?" John asked.

"I don't know," Jessica replied honestly.

"Now, will you tell me where and when?" John asked.

"Nope," Jessica replied. "Still don't trust you! Gotta go! Love you! Bye!" Jessica disconnected and John looked at the phone.

"I said I wouldn't be a part of your bust," John said out loud to no one. He sent a text, and a few seconds later, he got the information he wanted in return. "That doesn't mean I'm not going to watch," John said as he walked out of the room.

Chapter 78

"Bruce," a voice said through the fog and haze of the drugs that were being used to sedate him. "You have a visitor." Bruce forced his eyes open. His doctor was standing there with two armed guards. Standing behind them was his lawyer. A smile covered his lawyer's face. Bruce suspected this was going to be an interesting talk. Bruce looked at the doctor who he had come to hate during his incarceration.

"Thank you, Doctor," Bruce replied. "I will never forget," Bruce emphasized the words, "never forget." "The way you treated me while I was in your care," he finished. One of the guards instinctively reached for his gun, causing Bruce to laugh.

"I don't think it is necessary to treat my client that way," Arnold, Bruce's lawyer, said. The guard looked at the lawyer and then at Bruce. The guard moved his hand away from the gun but put it on the doctor's shoulder, leading him out of the room. As the guard left, he cast one more suspicious glance back to Bruce.

"I won't forget you either," Bruce said to the guard, grinning. The guard's eyes narrowed, and he looked at Bruce with pure venom. Arnold shut the door to break the staring contest between the two. The lawyer looked at his client with admiration. Arnold had been sent in by Archibald and company to make sure Bruce didn't implicate anyone in their little cabal. Arnold had quickly learned his client not only wouldn't implicate his bosses, but Bruce was still fighting. Bruce believed that one day, and soon, he would be a free man. Arnold had come to believe in Bruce as well and was willing to do anything that didn't cross his current clients to help him.

"What's the special occasion, Arnold?" Bruce asked. Arnold pulled himself from his thoughts. He smiled at his client.

"All the paperwork has been cleared," Arnold replied, beaming. "Between not being able to guarantee the safety of a former FBI agent, and your either diminished capacity, or insanity, the court's words, not mine," Arnold quickly added. Bruce smiled and nodded. Arnold continued. "You're going to a hospital instead of prison." Bruce was pleased; his biggest obstacle was over. He wasn't going to jail, and John was dead. Now, it was time to get out of this bed and begin to work on his plan to decimate the rest of John's team.

"Thank you," Bruce said simply. Arnold nodded, pleased with himself. Bruce continued. "I am going to need two things: physical therapy and some reading material." Arnold lifted an eyebrow.

"I've been working on getting you up and walking," Arnold replied. "But, the reading material will have to be approved. That might prove to be a little difficult. It's not that I can't do it; it's just going to take some time. Is there anything in particular that you're looking for?"

"I came very close to being killed," Bruce began with a huge grin on his face. "Do you think I can get some medical books, specifically dealing with spinal cord injuries and paralysis?" Arnold smiled.

"That may take some doing," Arnold began. He tapped his finger on his chin for a second while looking up at the ceiling. He got a sly smile on his face and looked back at Bruce. "Try this. My client has had a traumatic experience. After being shot and realizing the heinousness of his crimes, he would like to now spend his time helping others. He wants to learn how to help those who are less fortunate than him."

"I'd clap, Arnold," Bruce began but looked down at his hands and shrugged. Arnold laughed out loud. Bruce smiled. "Thank you, Arnold, and please let Archibald know that there's no hard feelings." Arnold nodded and left. The smile from Bruce's face fell. There were hard feelings, very hard feelings, but the first objective was to take care of Chet and Jessica. After that, then it would be time for Bruce to play.

"Should have stayed out of the FBI, John," Bruce said quietly. He began to laugh. After a few minutes, the doctors came in to give him something to calm him. As Bruce drifted off, he realized he was sad. He never got to see John's coffin lowered into the ground. He decided when he got out, he would dig it up just so he could rebury it.

Jeremiah Cosby
White House

Chapter 79

Jeremiah was leaving a very important meeting when one of the Secret Service men came up to him. Jeremiah was wondering if there was any meeting that wasn't important now that he was vice president. He had hoped to change America, but that was hard to do when emergencies he hadn't even known existed kept popping up all over the place. He wondered what this particular emergency was. The irritation of the day must have shown on his face because the agent told him before he even asked.

"It's Director Smothers, sir," the agent said. "He said you'll want to take this call." Jeremiah's face broke out in a grin.

"Trip, give me some good news ma'boy!" the vice president exclaimed into the phone after he swiped it out of the agent's hand.

"We've got him," Trip replied simply. Jeremiah began to do a jig right in the White House. The agent with him just looked to the ceiling.

"How bad?" Jeremiah asked.

"We've only got him on one charge, but it's enough," Trip replied. He paused and then told the part he had been dreading. "Brian Nichols is turning evidence against him." The smile fell from Jeremiah's face.

"Trip, I need you to do something for me," Jeremiah said seriously. "Make sure he has round the clock protection. You'll have to trust me on this one ma'boy."

"The US attorney and US Marshals have him, Jeremiah," Trip replied.

"I'll take care of it," he replied. Jeremiah paused and decided to go ahead and ask the question that was burning in his mind. "Anything on the other baby?"

"Dr. Nichols told Jessica that Sam's baby died," Trip replied somberly.

"Do you believe him?" Jeremiah asked. Trip barked a laugh.

"You're as bad as John," Trip replied. He was silent for a second, then continued. "I don't know. Part of me thinks I should send someone to the gravesite with ground penetrating radar just to see. John is so sure. He won't tell it, but it's obvious to everyone that he thinks the baby is alive."

"Do you think the old boy just wants to find one last connection to his dearly departed wife?" Jeremiah asked.

"I might have before the shooting, but now . . ." Trip trailed off. Jeremiah laughed.

"I've talked to Arthur and heard all about it," Jeremiah replied. Trip laughed.

"When did you two get so chummy?" Trip asked.

"Hold your tongue!" Jeremiah exclaimed but chuckled as well. "I have to go save the world, Trip. Let me know when you lock him up."

"I will sir," Trip replied. "And sir, thank you for the help on this one."

"Trip, I can honestly say it was all my pleasure," Jeremiah said and disconnected the call. He turned to the Secret Service agent that was with him. "Well, come on ma'boy. We've got a Congress to go upset." And with that, Jeremiah took off down the hall with his agents hurrying to follow after him.

Duck
Somewhere in Florida

Chapter 80

Duck was all alone in his office when his phone rang. He looked at the caller ID and saw it was blocked. It was probably a burner phone. Duck picked up the phone.

"Quack," he said.

"Just listen," the voice on the other end said. It was clearly Kenneth. "The doctor has been arrested and has turned evidence on our friend like we preplanned. I will take care of everything; however, it needs to be taken care of. You have not been named in anything. Do you understand?"

"Quack," Duck answered. The line disconnected. Duck got up and walked over to the map that was hanging on the wall in front of him. He walked back over to his desk and pressed a button. A light came out of the desk and showed on the map. It covered countries all over the world. The marks on the map were where Duck and his associates had shipped people to sell them into the black market. Some marks were where Duck's private airplane had landed with the doctor. The doctor had then delivered the babies of the slaves and sold the babies for profit. It would be a shame to lose the doctor, but it had to be done. They had all warned him of trying to make extra money here in the states.

Duck would begin the search tomorrow to find someone who could do the work overseas for them at a reasonable price. Duck was glad that Kenneth wasn't mad at him. Duck was a businessman first off, and if Brian wanted to make wagers and use up his current earnings and future earnings, then that was Brian's problem, not Kenneth's.

Duck walked back over to the desk and flicked off the switch, and the filled in parts of the map went away. He walked over to the window and looked out at the sky. He was getting quite tired of what was starting to become constant interference by the FBI. Maybe the time had come to do something that seemed a little drastic. Maybe it was time to get rid of what was left of John's team, and Director Smothers. He walked over to his phone and pushed a button. Less than a minute later, one of his men walked in.

"I want you to get in touch with our lawyer Arnold," Duck began. "I want you to have him ask his client if he is interested in getting rid of some loose ends. I think he will find the compensation more than fair." The man nodded but looked a little unsure. "Speak your mind."

"Why would Bruce agree to such a thing?" the made man asked.

"Why wouldn't he?" Duck replied, laughing. "That man is a psychopath. He enjoys killing. For him to take out our enemies would just be a happy coincidence. Wouldn't you say?" The made man smiled and nodded, understanding. He turned and left Duck by himself.

"It's time to end this mess," Duck said quietly to himself.

Chapter 81

Jessica looked at the group around her. Chet was ready to go. He had been waiting for this moment for years. She looked over at Ron. He might be a rookie in the FBI, but it was obvious this wasn't the first time he had prepared to go into a gun battle. She wondered if he would ever be willing to tell her what happened to him when he was in the armed forces. Not that it really mattered; after today, she would probably never work with him again. Jessica smiled at the thought of Ron and John working together. Talk about alpha dogs!

Jessica looked over all of the vehicles that continued to pull up. Her smile went to a look of slight confusion when she saw Trip get out of one of the SUVs. Trip came over to her, amused.

"Do you really think I'd miss this?" he asked. "Are we okay?" Jessica smiled and nodded her head.

"Like I said, Trip, I don't agree with the deal struck with Dr. Nichols, but there's a game being played at a level or ten above my pay grade. And, apparently, there's a game being played above our head with Archibald and his goons. Besides, I do kinda owe you for letting me talk to the doctor before they put him in protective custody." Trip stuck his hands in his pockets and barely nodded. Jessica smiled at him. "Do you want point?" she offered. Trip sighed and shook his head.

"This isn't mine," Trip said simply.

"It's not really mine either," Jessica replied. Trip nodded and glanced around. He looked back at Jessica. "He isn't here, is he?" Jessica looked astonished.

185

"John?!" she asked, slightly exasperated. Trip nodded. "He's still legally dead. None of these agents even knows he's alive except for Chet. He doesn't have clearance to drive. He has been told to stay away, given what he did to Archibald, and I told him I would personally hurt him if he shows up." Trip listened to everything Jessica had to tell him and just continued to stare at her. The smile slowly fell from her face as she thought. She looked around for a few seconds and then turned back to Trip, and spoke in a low, hurried voice. "No, I haven't seen him, but I'm going to go look around and make sure he's not here." As she walked off, she paused and turned back toward Trip.

"He really deserves to see this," she said simply. Trip nodded.

"I've got someone recording it for our protection if anything is brought up in court, so please make sure everything is by the book," Trip replied with a smirk on his face. Jessica smiled broadly and went to make sure John wasn't anywhere around. Trip surveyed everything. Trip suspected Archibald knew they were coming, and that was fine with Trip. Archibald had told Jessica that Sam and John had gotten exactly what they deserved. Trip thought Archibald deserved worse than what they were going to do to him, but for now, it was a start. He heard Jessica give the signal for everyone to go, and the agents began to take their positions as Trip joined Jessica on the way up to the house.

David George
Staples Residence

Chapter 82

David George was in his nest, gun trained on the
front door of the Staples mansion. Today was the day; he
knew it in his heart. Today was the day that Veronica paid
for what she did to him and his sister all those years ago.
He was so sure that today was the day of retribution, that it
took him by surprise when a fleet of SUVs approached
Archibald's compound. They set up a perimeter, and a
group of agents began to approach the house. David was
about to panic. He forced himself to calm down. Nothing
was going to deter him from today's mission. Especially
not the FBI without . . . wait. Another car had pulled up to
the front gate and was let inside. The car parked short of
the house, well behind the agents heading to the house, and
David saw a familiar figure get out of the passenger side.

David turned his binoculars to the figure and
smiled. David George saw someone walking around to the
back of the house. David thought there was a shooting
range there, but he wasn't completely sure. He checked his
supplies, and found his parabolic microphone. He moved
very carefully and pointed it down at the agents
surrounding the front of the house.

David listened for a second, and the smile fell off
his face. The FBI was there for Archibald. It sounded like
they didn't have anything on Veronica. David shook his
head, prepared his gun, and looked though the sight,
looking for his target, Veronica.

Archibald Staples
Staples Residence

Chapter 83

Archibald was in his office when Tank came running down the hall with the red cellphone. Archibald took the phone from Tank.

"Go ahead," he said into the phone.

"I have just received information from my person inside the DOJ," the voice on the other end of the phone said. Archibald recognized the voice as Kenneth's. "My father stuck to the prearranged story. He has only implicated you in this crime, and no others. However, the FBI is moving in on you as we speak to arrest you."

"One second," Archibald replied. He flicked a remote, and his 103 inch television changed from the TV show he was watching to the security camera feeds he had set up around the estate. Archibald saw all the FBI agents slowly moving across the property. "They're here, and they should be at my front door any second."

"Blast!" Kenneth exclaimed. "I was hoping you could get away."

"I still might be able to," Archibald replied. "They do not have the boat area secure. If I could get there, I could possibly get away. London?" There was silence for a second.

"London works," Kenneth replied. There was a pause on the line. Archibald didn't know how to ask the question that hung in the air. Kenneth broached the subject.

"Archibald," Kenneth began. "If you can't get away, then I will do as I promised. I will take care of this situation."

"I will get away if it is possible, but I'm not going to take a bullet for him," Archibald replied.

"I understand and agree," Kenneth replied. "Hopefully, I'll see you in London." With that, he disconnected. Archibald called in Tank. Tank came in, and saw the monitors and the red cellphone in Archibald's hand.

"I'll take care of it, sir," Tank said. Archibald shook his head.

"Just the phone, Tank. Just the phone," Archibald said, never averting his gaze from the monitors. He looked up at Tank. "This is what I was talking about earlier." Tank didn't look happy, but he nodded. Archibald heard his daughter yelling. She had obviously seen the FBI agents approaching the house. "Take care of the phone; I'll take care of her," he said to Tank. Tank nodded and left. Archibald steadied himself and went to calm his shrieking daughter.

"If I do get arrested," he said out loud to no one. "At least I won't have to listen to her for a while."

Chapter 84

Jessica, followed by Trip, Chet, Ron, and the rest of the agents, headed toward the front door. Some of Archibald's goons tried to stop them, or slow them up. Jessica couldn't tell which, but the agents showed them their badges, patted down the goons, and began to arrest any of them that were armed.

"You'd think he'd take the time to make sure they were carrying legal weapons, or be properly documented, as many times as the FBI has raided this place," Jessica said.

"It's all part of his arrogance," Trip replied. He smiled as he watched another goon cuffed and led away. Jessica reached the front door, and Archibald's men that were stationed there were promptly taken care of. She turned to Trip, smiling. Trip returned the smile and held his hand out to the door.

"Please, ladies first," Trip said.

"Don't mind if I do," she replied. She pounded on the door. "Archibald Staples!" she shouted. "This is the FBI! You are under arrest! Give yourself up, or we are coming in!" A second later, the door opened. Archibald walked forward and stopped when he was inside the door frame. He had a self-assured look on his face.

"Agent," he said to Jessica. "Why are you wasting your time arresting me? You know I'll be out in hours," he said, smugly. Jessica smiled.

"I don't care. Now raise your hands," she replied, wishing John was here to see this. Archibald raised his hands. It was at that moment that Veronica came barging out of the house. She pushed her father aside and barreled through the doorway, shrieking. She got in front of her father, yelling about the injustice of the FBI raiding her father's property. The agents backed up a little, and Veronica moved forward into the perfect kill zone. She turned slightly to the side to face Trip and scream at him. From his nest, David George smiled. Veronica had turned herself to where he now had a straight shot. With the current angle of the shot, no one would be hit but Veronica. David pulled the trigger. The pain and rage he had held all these years drained out of his body. He dropped the gun, got on his knees, and put his hands on his head, waiting to be discovered and taken into custody. Relief had filled his entire being. He was truly at peace.

At the manor, Veronica had suddenly stopped shrieking as a hole appeared in the front of her head. The bullet exited the back of her head and lodged into the doorway. Jessica, Chet, Trip, and Archibald were all covered with blood from the splatter of the gunshot. All the agents dropped, and spun toward where they thought the shot came from. Ron took charge; he quickly calculated where the shot had come from and prepared a team to take out the sniper. Archibald realized what had happened to his daughter but also knew that for a minute, no one would be paying attention to him. He took this as his opportunity to flee. Archibald brought his elbow up and forward, catching Jessica in the face as she turned back to face him. He knocked the gun out of her hand, grabbed her, and shoved her into Chet and Trip. He sprinted back through the house. Jessica got up quickly and began to chase him. Chet and Trip were trying to get up off the ground. As Archibald opened the back door to his home, he had an evil smile on his face. He closed the door and locked it, taking in one last look at his home. This would probably be the last time he would get to see it for some time. It was a shame his daughter was dead, but he could get away, and Kenneth had already said he would help him.

Archibald had it all mapped out. He would sprint past his shooting range and get to the boat house that was on his property. He had had a getaway planned for years and had practiced how to use it regularly. Archibald turned back around and ran up the stairs that emptied into the back of his property. When he cleared the stairwell and could see the boathouse in the distance, his mouth dropped as he came to a sudden stop. He saw what he thought was a dead man standing in front of him.

"Hello, scumbag," John said.

John Fowler, Fifteen Minutes Earlier
Staples Residence

Chapter 85

John and Arthur sat in the car that was parked off
the road. They were a little ways away from the Staples
estate. John was watching the festivities by the gate
through his binoculars. He hated lying to Jessica, but he
had to be here just in case Archibald tried something. Also,
he really, really wanted to see Archibald arrested. John
didn't believe Archibald would give up without a fight, and
he wanted to make sure everything was covered just in case
he was right.

"You know she's going to be mad at you," Arthur
said.

"Uh-huh," John replied, never taking his eyes from
the binoculars. Arthur chuckled.

"When are you going to marry her?" Arthur asked.
John swallowed.

"Why would you ask that?" John asked nervously.

"Because you had a near death experience and you
know either one of you could go at any minute," Arthur
replied. John lowered his binoculars and looked over at
Arthur.

"I always thought when people did things like that
after traumatic events, they usually broke up," John replied.
Arthur shrugged.

"You're not talking about starting a relationship
after an event. I think it's a different story if you take stock
of your life after an event like this and decide to make
changes." Arthur paused and then smiled. "It's not like
you haven't thought about it." John nodded solemnly.
Arthur patted John on the shoulder and let him go back to
his surveillance.

John noticed people beginning to move and had Arthur start the car. Once everyone began to move as a group to the house, John had Arthur drive up to the front gate. When they pulled up, John flashed his badge to one of the junior agents.

"Sir, you're dead." the agent said to John. John laughed.

"Deep cover," John replied. "I came out just to see this go down." The agent nodded, and John hopped out of the car. He winked at Arthur who turned the car around and drove off. Arthur would have loved to stay and watch, but he wasn't an agent, and even John couldn't pull that kind of rank.

John snuck around to the back of the house where the firing range was located. He located the doorway of the stairwell that led from the back of the house that he thought Archibald would take if he tried to escape. John leaned against the wall and waited. Hopefully, he would never see any action on his private assignment, but he was ready, just in case.

Ron and Chet
After David George Shot Veronica

Chapter 86

Chet untangled himself from Trip. Trip began to gather up a team to follow after Jessica, all while keeping low in case of another sniper shot. Chet hurried after Ron's team. Trip watched Chet go and wondered if changes were coming on his elite team.

Chet caught up to the team being led by Ron. Ron saw him and nodded his approval. They came to the spot where Ron believed the shot came from and spread out. David George was lying face down with his fingers locked behind his head. The agents began to cuff him. Ron walked over to the rifle and whistled in appreciation. One of the agents gingerly picked it up so as not to rub out any prints. Chet finally got a look at David George's face as the agents picked him up once he was secure.

"David George," Chet said to him. David nodded. "You got her to admit everything on live TV; you got the President of the United States to resign with what you did. Wasn't that enough? You couldn't let it go, could you?"

"Could you?" David asked him back. Chet shook his head sadly. The agents led him away, and Ron walked over to Chet.

"You've been in on the Bruce takedown, and now this one," Ron began. "Sounds like someone is trying to come out of his shell," Ron observed.

"We've got to push ourselves," Chet replied and started to walk away. Ron grabbed his arm to stop him.

"Look, I don't know you that well, but if you're trying to prove something to someone, you don't need to," Ron said. "You're one of the greatest computer experts alive. I respect you, and I've fought all over the world."

"I let John get shot," Chet replied. "I let John get shot because I hung back. If I had been better trained, I would have made sure Bruce was dead or restrained him. I didn't, and John took a bullet through the chest, so either I have to get better in the field, or I have to completely stay out of the field. No one will say that to my face, but that's what they have to be thinking." Ron nodded.

"Then, let me help you," Ron offered. Chet thought about it and had a questioning look on his face.

"You live in Miami," Chet reminded him. Ron shook his head.

"No, I'm going to New York, with or without the FBI's help," Ron responded. Chet nodded and stuck out his hand. Ron grabbed it and clapped him on the shoulder with his other hand. "Let's head down. Apparently, they caught him," Ron said in response to the commotion that was going on down at the mansion.

Chapter 87

Archibald couldn't believe who he was seeing standing in front of him, smirking.

"You're dead!" he exclaimed. John shrugged.

"I got better," John replied. Archibald glared at John. John grinned even broader. It was time to bring Archibald to justice.

"I told you I'd bring you down if it was the last thing I did," John said as he punched Archibald right in his jaw. Archibald fell to the ground. He shook his head and growled like a crazed dog. In the past few minutes, Archibald had seen his daughter killed, and now, his sworn enemy that he thought was dead and buried, stood before him. Archibald snapped and dove at John's legs, pushing both men further out into the grounds. John's chest hurt, and he was short of breath. More importantly, he never thought Archibald could take a punch. John was surprised at Archibald's reaction. John had badly miscalculated what Archibald would do in this situation. John knew that in his condition, he was out-matched. As they both stood, John was more unsteady than Archibald. John accepted that he was in no shape for a fair fight. It was dirty, but he knew there was only one thing he could do. John kicked Archibald squarely in the groin. Archibald dropped to his knees, and John connected with a right cross to Archibald's jaw. Archibald toppled over. John heard the back door swing open and footsteps coming up the steps. John was trying to psyche himself up for another fight with one of Archibald's goons when Jessica stepped out. John couldn't tell if she was mad or not, but he thought he was about to find out, right after he fell on the ground.

John began to sway a little when he noticed the blood on Jessica. Adrenaline rushed through him at seeing the blood. He glanced over Jessica quickly and noticed no noticeable injuries. John decided he needed to appear to be in control of his faculties. He got a pair of cuffs out of his jacket pocket and began to cuff Archibald.

"Did he do that to you?" John asked. Jessica shook her head.

"Someone shot Veronica," Jessica said. John had been looking down as he was cuffing Archibald. When hearing the news about Veronica, he jerked his head up and stared at Jessica. "She's dead, John. The bullet went right through her head." John looked away for a second. He never wanted to see the loss of life, but the simple fact was Veronica had killed someone because of who she was. John looked down at Archibald.

"I blame you," John said quietly. "You made her this way." Archibald could only groan. John smiled and stood. He then noticed a cut on Jessica's cheek and some bruising. "What happened?" he asked her.

"Archibald got in a lucky shot," she replied, staring daggers at Archibald. John shook his head and kicked Archibald in the gut. Jessica looked at John in horror.

"You can't do that!" she exclaimed. John shrugged.

"Why not?" he asked. "I'm currently dead, so he can't press charges. Besides, he hurt my girl." Jessica cocked her head to the side and gave him an exasperated look.

"Do you think that will hold up in court?" Jessica asked. John shrugged and tried to get Archibald up to his feet. John realized the rush of adrenaline was over, and he didn't have the strength. In fact, he really felt like a nap right then. John went down to one knee, and Jessica came over to him. She reached down tenderly. She pulled his head up to make sure he was alright. When she realized he was okay, the biggest grin covered her face.

"You have been shot," Jessica said, enjoying the moment.

"I seem to keep getting reminded of that at the most inopportune moments," he replied. "Do you mind?" John asked, gesturing towards Archibald. Jessica smiled and tried to drag Archibald to his feet. He made one more attempt to get away by crashing into Jessica, driving her to the ground. John started to run over to her when he realized what was going on. Jessica had her left arm wrapped around Archibald's neck under his throat, choking him out. His arms were handcuffed to each other behind his back, so he couldn't fight back. Archibald started to squirm, and Jessica looked over at John and smiled. She then arched backwards, and John could hear Archibald's muffled yells die down as the oxygen was driven out of him. Jessica let him go, and Archibald toppled off her to the ground. Jessica got up and stood over him.

"Are you done?" she asked. Archibald nodded. She helped him up and marched him through the house, and back outside the front door. John followed slowly, making a mental note of what he had just seen.

"Look who I found," she said to the agents working on Veronica's dead body.

"We're going to need that shirt, ma'am," one of the techs said. John appeared in the doorway.

"Are you trying to get fresh with my girlfriend?" John asked the tech. The tech quickly shook her head. Trip groaned at the whole exchange.

"Where did you find that?" Trip said, pointing at Archibald.

"It appears Archibald's face ran into this private citizen's fist, and at some point, it seems Archibald's groin ran into the citizen's foot," Jessica replied. Trip and the other males at the scene made a face and an "uhhn" noise.

"John," Trip simply said, while shaking his head.

"If anyone ever deserved it . . . " John trailed off and just nodded toward Archibald. Trip thought and then nodded in agreement.

Chapter 88

Ron and Chet came back from chasing down the sniper and joined the group. David George was being led off in chains. John walked over closer to get a look at him. John had to admit that for the first time since he had met David George, the man seemed at peace. John shook his head and looked over toward Veronica's body.

"Such a waste," Trip said as he had walked up behind John.

"There was only one way he was ever going to get closure," John replied. Trip nodded. They both stood there a second, thinking about the first time they had seen David led away. After a second, Trip clapped John on the shoulder.

"Come on," Trip said. "There's someone I want you to meet."

Trip walked John over to Chet, Jessica, and Ron.

"John, this is Ronald McGuire," Trip said.

"I thought you were dead," Ron blurted out. He closed his eyes and silently chided himself. He opened his eyes quickly, and John was smiling.

"I get that a lot," John replied. "I got better. It's good to meet you, Ronald."

"Just Ron if you don't care," Ron said, extending his hand. John shook it.

"Nice to meet you, Just Ron," John replied. Ron smiled a little uncomfortably, Chet rolled his eyes, and Jessica sighed and then kicked John in the shin. Ron was getting more uncomfortable by the minute. As John hopped, Jessica tried to explain.

"John has a little trouble," Jessica said to Ron. "He has the worst case of being an idiot any of us has ever seen." Ron didn't look any less nervous.

"They're dating," Chet said to Ron.

"Chet, you're not supposed to say that in front of Trip," John said, still trying to put weight on the leg Jessica kicked. "That makes Trip nervous." John turned toward Jessica. "I was shot."

"I know," she replied. "I was there." Trip stood there with his right hand over his face. His thumb was under his right eye with his index finger running up his nose, while his other three fingers curved to cover his mouth. He was looking up at the sky. He seemed to be mumbling something that sounded like, "Why me?"

"Are you two finished with your performance?" Trip asked, removing his hand from his face. Jessica, with a questioning look on her face, turned to Chet.

"Did you tell him when the bust was going down?" she asked Chet directly. Chet, ignoring Jessica, turned toward Ron.

"Are you playing online tonight?" Chet asked Ron. Jessica put her hands on her hips and shot Chet a look. Chet smiled at Jessica and turned back to Ron. Ron nodded. "You've got my ID, right?" Ron nodded again, somewhat nervous to speak. John raised an eyebrow.

"You play computer games?" John asked Ron. Ron nodded. "What did you do before the FBI?" John asked, wondering if Ron could speak.

"Special forces," Ron answered. John was taken aback.

"Oh, really," John replied. "Where were you stationed?"

"I can't tell you, sir," Ron replied with a grin on his face. "It's classified."

John smiled at Ron. He turned toward Trip. "Congrats, Trip." John turned toward Ron to watch him as he spoke. "I know you've always wanted someone from the Unit." Trip winced, Chet chuckled, and Jessica shook her head. Ron was confused.

"I never said I was Delta Force," Ron replied. Trip closed his eyes and shook his head. John smiled and turned back to Trip.

"This is a big win for you," John continued. "Usually Langley ends up with these guys." John turned back to Ron. "Just so you know, the guy you apprehended earlier was part of the 5th Special Forces Group." John saw a momentary flicker of sorrow in Ron's eyes. "The woman he killed had his sister killed years ago." Ron glanced over at the body of Veronica and back to John.

"That's unfortunate," Ron said simply. John nodded solemnly. Ron stood there for a second, looking frustrated and then finally asked, "Why do you keep insisting I'm part of Delta Force?" Trip chuckled.

"John has this ability," Trip began. "He was fishing to start with, but when you responded to his question, he was able to read you, for lack of a better word." Ron was astonished. He turned toward John.

"That's amazing! How long did you have to study?" Ron asked.

"Not a day in his life," Jessica responded, half annoyed. "I know it's cool right now, but it can be the most annoying thing in the world if you have to work with him long." Trip and Chet laughed, while Ron looked at John confused. John just shrugged.

Chapter 89

John watched Chet and Jessica with Ron. He turned toward Trip.

"Do we still have those openings?" John asked. Trip, looking a little surprised, nodded. John turned back to Ron.

"Were you looking for an assignment in a particular city?" he asked Ron. Ron nodded his head yes, a little confused. "What do you think of these two?" John asked. Ron paused, picking his words carefully.

"They both have unique qualities," Ron replied. John frowned. "Ok, it was an absolute pleasure to work with a computer expert like Chet." John turned to Chet.

"He's got skill," Chet replied. John nodded and turned back to Ron.

"And Jessica?" he asked. Ron looked at Jessica. Jessica crossed her arms and raised an eyebrow. Ron visibly swallowed.

"The stories about her don't do her justice, sir," Ron replied softly. "I hope I'm never on the other side of any interrogation with her. She only said three words to the guy in the box, and he admitted everything!!" John threw back his head and roared with laughter. Trip and Chet turned away because they were laughing so hard. Even Jessica had to laugh. "Did I miss something?" Ron asked. John turned to Trip and nodded. Trip extended his hand to Ron.

"I'd like you to come work in New York," Trip said. Ron smiled and shook his hand, accepting the offer. "And, yes, Ron, you did miss something. We'll explain it all one day, but the short story is Jessica once interrogated John. In the meantime, I'd like you to fill in for John until he returns to active duty. Jessica will run the team, but I believe one day that you may have your own." Ron looked conflicted.

"Go ahead, Agent," Trip said to Ron.

"Can I stay on the team when John comes back?" Ron asked. John raised his eyebrows in surprise. He looked over at Trip.

"Your call, John," Trip responded.

"Let's see how you feel when I come back and after a few assignments working with me," John offered. Ron nodded, smiling. He turned to go, and Chet went with him. Jessica walked and put her hand on John's shoulder. Trip turned toward John.

"He won't last two cases with you," Trip said. Jessica shook her head.

"I don't know Trip; he's good," she said, simply.

"Why did he leave Delta Force?" John asked. Jessica stepped back and looked at him. "He doesn't look that old," John pointed out. Trip turned to John.

"Don't," Trip said simply. "Just don't." John nodded. Trip walked off. Jessica grabbed John's hand and squeezed it.

"You're going to, aren't you?" she asked. John sighed.

"I'll leave it alone if I can," John replied. Jessica smiled and gave him a quick kiss. John smiled at her. "Can you give me a ride back to Arthur's?" John asked. "He said we'd take a helicopter ride back to New York if I was ready to go home, and I am." Jessica nodded. She looked at John and found the courage to tell him what she had learned.

"John," she began. "I interviewed Dr. Nichols about Sam's baby. He said Sam's baby was dead." John listened, and when Jessica finished, he looked away. He looked at the river that was flowing behind the mansion. He didn't want to argue with Jessica, but he wondered. His mind wouldn't let go of the hope that some small part of Sam might be out there. He knew he had to let go. He had let Sam go when he came back from whatever had happened a few weeks ago, and now, he needed to let go

205

the hope that her child survived. He sighed, smiled, and turned back to Jessica.

"Are you okay?" she asked. John nodded.

"Do you mind giving me that ride now?" he asked. Jessica nodded.

"Do you want me to go to New York with you right now?" she asked. John shook his head no.

"You've got some work to do," he replied, smiling at Jessica. "I'm okay with this; really, I am. I was just hoping, you know?" Jessica smiled at him.

"I know," she replied. She sighed. I do have a lot of paperwork to do on this case. Call you later?" John nodded. They walked to Jessica's vehicle as John looked back over Archibald's home. John smiled. They had brought Archibald down. That had to count for something today. John saw Trip and waved bye. Trip did something unusual. He yelled.

"Sam would be proud," he bellowed at John. John smiled and got in the vehicle. Sam would be proud, but John didn't think this was over. There was still one more person to capture. John sighed. How was he going to find something on the former president? He didn't have the answer, but he knew he needed to heal first, and then, he would deal with Kenneth Nichols.

John Fowler, The Next Day
New York, New York

Chapter 90

John sat in his apartment, knowing he was supposed to take it easy. He thought he should be out celebrating. Archibald was in jail. John was sure Archibald would figure some way out, sooner rather than later, but for now, he was paying for his crimes. John thought that should have made him happy, but it didn't. He got up and looked out over the city, Sam's city. It would always be hers. John knew he was feeling cooped up and bored, but he had felt that way during his days as a private investigator. This was something different. John was lonely, but he wasn't lonely for Sam. John felt like he had a family again. He and his parents had repaired all of their problems. They were coming to New York soon to visit him. John was honestly surprised his mother hadn't chewed him out for having to fake his own death, but when Jessica explained it all to her, his mom took it fine. That had been one of the strangest phone calls he had ever been a part of. Four people: him, Jessica, his mother, and his father, all on the phone at once.

John had to admit that his relationship with the Moores was the best it had probably ever been. His relationship with Trip was definitely the best it had ever been, and he and Chet were back to being themselves. John knew that he would have to get to know Ron. No matter what Trip said, he didn't see Ron leaving the team any time soon.

John had to face the 800 pound gorilla in the room. He and Jessica had never been closer, and it wasn't enough for John. When she first walked into his apartment some time back after John asked Chet if he thought John was suicidal, Jessica had told him no. John wasn't so sure, but he was sure now. He had faced death and the possibility of being reunited with Sam, but it wasn't enough for him. He told Sam he chose Jessica, but what had he really done? John turned his neck to crack it. Was he really considering what was dancing in the corners of his mind? Did John really want to go down that road again? John looked over at his phone. He started to pick it up twice, and both times, he set it down. No, he decided. If he was going to do this, he was going to do it right.

Chapter 91

Thirty minutes later, John and Chet stood in a jewelry store. John thought he might hyperventilate any second. Chet looked a little concerned.

"Maybe we should slow down," Chet said. "You're only about three weeks out from being shot." John shook his head.

"I'm in pretty good shape," John answered. "I just get tired, and I'm going to be fighting that for months. No, Chet. What's bothering me has nothing to do with being shot. What if she says no?"

"Then, you're where you're at right now," Chet responded. "Ask yourself this; what if she says yes?" John thought for a second and got a goofy grin on his face. Chet sighed and began to look around. After two sales people and an hour of looking, John settled on a ring.

"If she should happen to say no, you can bring it back, sir," the saleslady said. Chet shot her a death look. The saleslady caught the look and then glanced at John. "I'm sure that won't be the case, sir," she said. Chet sighed and stared up at the ceiling. John looked like a deer in headlights as Chet led him out of the store.

"She might say no?" John asked. Chet shook his head.

"No way, buddy," he replied. "Not in a million years. Where to?" John didn't answer. "Jessica's?"

John nodded, never speaking. It took several minutes to get across town, and Chet didn't know what to say. The entire ride was filled with silence. When they arrived at Jessica's, John opened the door, looked over at Chet, and nodded. John got out of the car and started into Jessica's building. Chet watched his friend go inside. He didn't know whether to laugh at him or not.

John took the elevator up to her floor, trying to think of what to say to Jessica, but nothing came to mind. John got out of the elevator and walked down the hall, his mind still blank. John stood in front of Jessica's door, trying to decide what to say. He gave up and walked down the hall, preparing to leave. He then turned back around, determined to propose. After a couple of minutes of this, he steadied himself.

  "John, you're being a fool," he said to himself. "You love her, and she loves you. If she says no, then she says no." John went to the door and raised his hand to knock.

Chapter 92

John knocked on Jessica's door. After a few seconds, Jessica opened the door, saw John, and looked worried.

"John, we don't have a date tonight, do we?" Jessica asked frantically. "I am so sorry. You know how busy I've been with the case. Give me a few minutes to get ready." John smiled at Jessica.

"Any chance I can come in?" John asked. Jessica realized she had not even invited John inside and was blocking the doorway. She smiled, moved to the side of the door, and made a sweeping gesture for John to enter. John stepped through the doorway, and kissed Jessica. The kiss lasted for a little bit, when John broke it, his lips were inches from hers.

"I guess you've forgiven me for forgetting our date?" Jessica asked coyly.

"We didn't have any plans tonight that I can remember," John replied, shutting the door behind them.

"Mr. Fowler," Jessica said smiling. "You just show up at my door and think you can," Jessica couldn't finish the sentence because John was kissing her again. She pulled away and looked deep into his eyes. "Is something wrong?"

"Yeah," John replied. "I died, Jess. I died, and I realize that this life is way too short. I go home, and you're not there. I wake up, and you're not there. I go to sleep, and you're not there."

Jessica smiled, "Baby, that would kind of go against the ground rules we set up," she gently reminded him. John grinned, the same grin he always got when he knew something that no one else did. Jessica grinned back. "Maybe you're thinking of breaking our rules, but I haven't agreed to." John grinned even broader. "Don't forget John. You're injured, and I can out fight you even when

211

you're 100%," John laughed and began to sink to one knee. Jessica's jaw dropped. "John, what are you doing?"

"What does it look like Jessica?" John asked on one knee.

"It looks like you're about to propose," Jessica replied.

"There's a reason you're a master detective, Jess," John said, reaching into his coat pocket and pulling out a box. John opened the box, and inside was an engagement ring.

"Jessica Louise," John began.

"How did you find out my middle name?!?" Jessica interjected.

"Will you marry me?" John asked, ignoring Jessica's outburst. Jessica smiled and began to cry. She looked at the ring and then at John. She helped John to his feet, smiling with tears streaming down her cheeks. Jessica kissed John. When she broke the kiss, she gently put her forehead on his.

"No," she replied softly.

Chapter 93

Jessica took both of John's hands into hers. For John, that was probably best because he was about to pass out. He was sure Jessica would say yes. He looked into her eyes. The eyes staring back at him were of someone who loved him. John didn't understand.

"You're just messing with me, right?" John asked.

"No, baby, I'm not," Jessica replied. "I love you."

"I love you," John replied. "I don't see where that's a problem with us getting married."

"You're not ready," Jessica replied simply. She kissed him on the nose, dropped his hands, and headed toward the kitchen. "Do you want something to eat?"

John stood there for a second, thinking Jessica was even crazier than he realized. He shook his head and walked into the kitchen.

"Look," John began but noticed Jessica had her head in the refrigerator looking for food. "I'll make you a deal. Answer me why you won't marry me, with a real answer, and I'll take you out to dinner."

Jessica straightened and squinted her eyes, thinking. "Delivery?" she counter offered.

"Deal," John said, exasperated.

"John, it's not that I don't want to marry you. I want nothing more, but you're not ready," she replied simply. John looked dumbfounded.

"Well, I just asked," John said. "How can I not be ready?"

"You just think we should get married," Jessica replied. She opened the freezer and pulled out a carton of ice cream, shut the freezer door, and turned back toward John. "Cookie dough?" she asked.

John looked at the ice cream and thought about how long it had been since he had had any cookie dough ice cream. He then realized Jessica was distracting him. He crossed the distance between them, took the ice cream out of her hands, and placed it on the counter. He then leaned into her and kissed her as passionately as he knew how.

Jessica's back pressed against the refrigerator door as John leaned into her. Jessica was afraid they were going to melt the ice cream and then decided she didn't care if they melted it or not. Jessica wrapped her arms around John's neck. She pulled away for a second and looked into John's eyes. She had never seen anyone look at her that way before, and she shivered. She kissed John; she kissed him so hard that she was sure she heard her back pop. She pulled away, breathless.

"John, we've got to stop," she said.

"Absolutely," John said, nodding. He was still nodding as he leaned in and began kissing her neck.

Jessica pushed him away, not really wanting to. "We need to stop," she said.

"We could get married," he replied. Jessica grabbed his head with both hands and looked him right in the eyes.

"There is nowhere we could get married tonight," Jessica replied.

"We could in the morning," John replied and then leaned in and kissed her gently. Jessica pulled away.

"And what about tonight?" she asked and then returned to kissing him. John pulled away, nearly groaning.

"We go back to our respective corners?" John asked. He began to kiss her again, and Jessica put her hand against his mouth.

"Stop," she said, very determined.

Chapter 94

Jessica shooed John back. She straightened her clothes, opened a drawer, and pulled out four delivery menus. She turned toward John with the menus spread out like a fan. John started to reach, and she pulled them away looking at him, exasperated. John blew out a sigh and covered his eyes with his hand. Jessica mixed the menus up and held them back up.

"Go ahead," she said. John reached out and picked one. Jessica looked at it, asked John if he wanted the usual, to which he nodded his head, and called to place an order. John grabbed a bottle of water out of the fridge and went and slumped onto Jessica's couch. Jessica finished the order, came out to the couch, and sat down beside John. She picked up his arm and snuggled up against him, placing his arm around her.

"Just because you think I'm insanely hot and my lease is about to run out is no reason for you to propose," Jessica said quietly. John popped up after she made the statement, causing Jessica to fall over into the couch corner. John didn't notice; he was too upset, pacing. He began to talk very loudly.

"You think this is about leases!?!" John exclaimed. "Jessica, I. LOVE! YOU! Beginning and end of story. I died and came back! You are the reason I decided to live. Were you not listening when I told you that? I was dead, Jess. I was dead and I was gone, but I couldn't do to you what Sam did to me. I couldn't Jess. Either one of us could die at any moment at our job. Let's be honest, neither one of us is ever going to give up doing what we do. I want you in my life every possible second; that's what I'm asking Jess. I'm asking you to be in my life, as short or as long as it is, for whatever remains of it." John finally turned toward Jessica and noticed her lying on the couch where she had fallen when he had hopped up. John pointed toward himself, "I did that, didn't I?" Jessica nodded.

John helped her sit up and then Jessica stood up. Her nose was an inch from his.

"You still love her," Jessica said very quietly.

"I'm always going to love her, just like I'm always going to love you, Jess," John replied. Jessica turned and walked a few steps away. She turned around to face John, looking him right in the eye. Her face was very determined.

"I'm not picking up after you," she replied.

"I think you picked up enough messes in my life," he replied softly.

"I'm not going to be your personal cook," she said.

"Will you at least call for delivery?" he asked, beginning to grin.

"Maybe," she replied with a grin of her own.

"I'll always be an alcoholic," John said solemnly.

"I can handle it," Jessica replied, crossing her arms over her chest.

"I'll drive you absolutely crazy, and I don't mean that in a good way," he said.

"I know," she replied, the grin returning. "But, you will drive me crazy in a good way too." Jessica crossed the space between them and hugged John. He held her for a minute.

"I've made my decision," she said softly.

"Do you want to reconsider?" John asked.

"Nope," Jessica replied, looking at him. "I don't want an engagement at this time in my life."

"Are you sure I can't change your mind?" John asked, trying to kiss her neck.

"No, John," Jessica replied, pushing him away. "When dinner comes, you pay for it, eat, and go home."

Chapter 95

The delivery came; John paid for it, ate, and got up to leave. He stopped in Jessica's doorway.

"You sure you want me to leave?" John asked. Jessica walked up behind him with her hand covering his on the door.

"No," Jessica said. John turned towards her. He kissed her gently on the lips, and moved their hands off the door. He broke the kiss and backed out the door, shutting it behind him.

"Lock the door," John said through the door.

"You have a key," Jessica replied.

"Don't remind me." Jessica locked the door and leaned up against it.

"I love you, John," she said softly.

"I love you, Jess. Good night," he said. Jessica listened for a minute.

"John, you need to go home," Jessica said.

"I know," he replied and left.

Jessica got on her cell and made a few phone calls. She called a judge she had gotten to know personally because she worked for the FBI. What John hadn't thought of was the fact that it might be hard to get married considering he was still dead. Jessica got a judge to sign off on the marriage and to waive the 24 hour waiting period. Jessica looked at her watch and decided it wasn't too late to call. She called the preacher of the church that Sam and John had attended. She had wanted to call Bro. Cobb, but he was back in Kentucky, and Jessica knew he could never make it to New York in time. The preacher she did call agreed to meet Jessica and John at 9:00 a.m. at John's apartment tomorrow. She then called John's parents and told them her plan, which they were all for. Jessica made three more quick calls. Jessica smiled as she sat her alarm for 3 a.m. She got into bed. She thought she would toss and turn all night. Jessica had never wanted a big fancy wedding. That was probably best because at this point, she was getting married tomorrow wearing something that was currently in her closet. As she drifted off to sleep, she wondered if John had understood what she had been saying to him earlier. He probably didn't, but that was ok. John didn't understand half the things anyone had ever told him.

Chapter 96

John woke up with a start. He was a little groggy and not for sure what was going on, but he was sure he heard something moving in his apartment. John reached over to the nightstand drawer and quietly opened it. He pulled his gun from the drawer, and slowly and quietly, got out of bed. He crept to the doorway. He paused. He slept in just a pair of shorts, and he wondered if he should put something else on. He decided against it and began to exit the room when he heard a voice.

"Put your gun away, and for the love of God, put some pants on!" Jessica yelled. John looked irritated. He went and put the gun away, got a tee shirt and a pair of cloth drawstring pants, and put them on. He walked into the kitchen. He glanced at the clock. It read 4:12.

"What are you doing?" John asked. Jessica turned around, smiled, walked over to him and kissed him deeply. John felt one of his knees give. Jessica broke the kiss, grinning like a Cheshire cat. On the stove was a skillet and a couple of eggs.

"I thought I'd make you breakfast before our big day," she said. "Do you have a suit that doesn't scream FBI?"

"Yeah," John replied, very confused.

"Good. Go take a shower and change into it. Chet and Trip will be here in a little while, although Trip isn't really happy about knowing what's going on." Jessica paused and turned toward John who was utterly confused. "I guess it will be ok if I don't have a bridesmaid. I could put a picture of Sam beside me, but that's just too weird. Trip caved when I asked if he would give me away." She paused again and pursed her lips. "I know I said I didn't want an engagement, but can I still wear the ring?"

Chapter 97

John was trying to put everything together, but as normal, when it came to the opposite sex, his mind was blown. He had finally noticed that Jessica was wearing a white dress. He noticed that flowers were arranged in the living room that weren't there when he went to bed the night before. John was struggling with what was going on. He thought he knew, but after Jessica had rejected him last night, he didn't dare hope he was right. Jessica was smiling, almost evilly. John shook his head, grinning.

"I guess, technically, since I didn't say yes last night, this needs to be done." Jessica got down on one knee and took John's hand. John looked away, completely embarrassed. She tugged on his hand. John looked down and saw Jessica looking back at him, love filling her eyes. John knew he should let her have this moment. John also knew that their relationship wasn't traditional in any sense of the word and decided he wasn't going to play fair. He got down on one knee in front of her. Jessica smiled broadly.

"John Edward Fowler," she began.

"Jessica Louise Hammerstein," John countered. Jessica's smile warmed his heart and caused it to speed up.

"Will you marry me?" she asked.

"Only if you'll marry me," he countered.

"I will," she replied and leaned in to kiss him. John stopped her and she raised an eyebrow.

"Thank you for taking care of things for me the past few years. Thank you for being Sam's friend. Thank you for being you, an incredible, smart, funny, witty, and jaw-droppingly beautiful woman." Jessica raised her eyebrows twice, very quickly, and kissed him deeply. This time, John didn't stop her. After a few seconds, he pulled away enough to talk to her.

"How long until everyone gets here?" John asked. Jessica responded by smacking the tip of his nose. "Ow!! What was that for!?" Jessica gave him a withering look.

"We will be married by noon today, John," she replied, irritated. "And then," she paused, and when she resumed, she spoke very softly. "I'll prove to you the wait has been worth it."

"While I'm sure it is," John began. "I only asked because I was wondering how much time we had to get everything ready before everyone gets here." Jessica looked slightly embarrassed.

"So, you weren't trying to --" she trailed off while circling her fingers and finally pointing at the bedroom. John shook his head, laughing.

"No. I wasn't trying to . . . I mean, I'm not saying I don't want to--" John paused as he noticed Jessica's eyebrow raising and he imagined her whacking his nose again. He stopped talking, stood up, and headed back toward his bedroom to shower. As he walked away he called back to her. "I'm going to take a shower before I get beat on anymore." Jessica watched him walk away.

"John," she called after him. John stuck his head out of the bedroom door, smirking. He was preparing a line about how she couldn't be without him, but she spoke first, and what she said took the smile from his face.

"My ring?" she asked while pointing at her finger. John groaned and disappeared into the bedroom. A second later, a ring box flew through the air. Jessica grabbed it, opened it, and put it on her finger. She held up her hand, admiring it. She looked around, wondering if she might see Sam. She didn't, but she spoke as if she was there anyway.

"I never thought I'd see this day," she said, lowering her hand. She put her hands on her knees. "I love you sweetie, and I miss you. I'll take care of him. I promise." Jessica swore she felt Sam hugging her from behind. Jessica brought her hand up to where Sam's arms would have crossed and sat there for a few minutes, knowing she had her friend's approval and blessing.

Chapter 98

Jessica heard a knock on the door and got up to see who it was. Trip and Chet were both there. Jessica let them in. She hugged Trip.

"Thank you," she said simply. She let Trip go, and she saw a tear in his eye. "Trip--," he cut her off.

"Don't start crying," he replied. "If you start that, Chet will start, and then, things will get really embarrassing."

"We can't have that now, can we?" John said, stepping from the bedroom. Jessica turned around and gave a low whistle when she saw him. John grinned. "Like what you see?"

"Do I?" she replied, walking towards him.

"Do you want us to leave you two alone?" Chet asked.

"NO!" the two yelled together, causing Trip and Chet to jump back in surprise. John and Jessica glanced at each other and both started laughing nervously. Trip had a smile on his face, while Chet just walked away shaking his head.

"It's not that we don't trust ourselves," Jessica began.

"Obviously, we're grown adults," John offered. Jessica nodded and continued.

"It's just we have a lot to do, and we can get sidetracked," Jessica said, while giving Trip the evil eye as he fought, unsuccessfully, to keep a grin off his face.

"Right," Trip said slyly. "What can we do?" For the few hours the four set about getting everything ready for the wedding. A courier arrived at eight A.M. with the documents necessary for the wedding. There was another knock on the door a few minutes later. John opened the door, expecting the minister. He was shocked when he saw Arthur and Madeline. John stood in the doorway for a second, not sure what to say.

"I know it's a big day, John," Arthur began. "But, would it be too much to ask us inside?" John quickly invited them in. Jessica was smiling ear to ear.

"I don't understand," John said. Arthur chuckled and turned to Trip.

"To be a great detective he can be quite dumb, can't he?" Arthur asked Trip. Trip roared with laughter. Arthur turned back to John, still stunned. "You need two witnesses, and Chet and Trip really shouldn't technically know this is happening, so that's where we come in. Well, that, and we made Jessica promise us that if you two ever got married, we could be there. Sam loved both of you, and there is no one she'd rather you both be with." John stood speechless. There was another knock on the door; this time, it was the minister. After a couple of minutes of introduction, everyone took their place, and the wedding began.

Chapter 99

"Dearly beloved," the minister began. John couldn't help but think back to his first wedding. This one was so much smaller and less of a social affair. Jessica was smiling the entire time. John was listening to the minister, but concentrating more on his future bride. That all changed when the minster asked John if he had prepared vows.

"What?" he asked, completely in shock. Jessica patted his hand.

"It's okay, baby," she said. "I thought maybe you'd like to say something, but if not, it's fine."

"You've got something prepared, don't you?" he asked. She grinned and nodded. John ran his hand over his face, causing Jessica to fight back laughter. John grinned as he looked around at his friends. He nodded and turned to face her.

"Ok," he began. "Here goes nothing. It's easy to care and love for someone when life is easy, and life is good. It's easy to talk about always and forever when there are no obstacles in front of you. Four years ago, I didn't know who I was, or what I stood for anymore. I felt it was my fault a man lost his life and I felt it was my fault my best friend, and yours Jessica, died." Jessica was nodding at him with tears in her eyes. "Through my entire meltdown, you did everything you could for me. You knew me, and you knew what I stood for even when I didn't. You saved me. I can talk all day long about what Sam would have done, but she didn't. You did. I can never thank you enough for that. I will forever be loyal to you. I will forever be your friend, and I will forever love you. That's all I can promise, but if it's enough, I want to spend every remaining day I have with you." Jessica had tears streaming down her face. "Jessica, will you marry me?"

"I will," she replied, smiling.

"Where did that come from?" Trip whispered to Chet, so John wouldn't hear him.

"I didn't know he had that in him," Chet replied, just as quiet. John cut the two of them a look, grinning.

"It's hard being me sometimes," John deadpanned. Everyone erupted in laughter. Jessica used the moment to wipe away all the tears. She took his hands.

"What can I say?" Jessica began. "No one knows better than me what I'm getting in to." John nodded at that, grinning. "You're right. I was there when Sam was gone and you were a mess. You had lost your way, but I did know what you were, and what you are about, and despite that," she paused as everyone chuckled. "Despite that," she continued, her voice a little softer. "I found that I couldn't get you out of my mind. I think some might consider the way I checked up on you for the last four years to be stalking." John chuckled, and Jessica smiled at him. "I've been without you for four years, and I didn't know someone could make me hurt like that. John, I can't imagine you not being in my life, and frankly, I want you in my life. I want you to drive me crazy and be the guy who catches the bad guys. I want to be so frustrated with you because all you care about is finding justice, finding peace for those who've lost someone, and finding the truth, no matter how bad it is some days. That is John Fowler. He's maddening, frustrating, charming, and heaven help me, I love him and always will." Jessica paused and thought she saw a tear in John's eyes. She smiled at him coyly. "How about it, John? Will you spend the rest of your life with me and drive me crazy in good and bad ways?"

"Yeah," John said softly. "I will." He started to lean in to kiss her when the minister "harrumphed," and John jerked back. Jessica grinned at him, and Trip put a hand on his shoulder to hold him back.

"Easy, boy," Trip said, grinning. John turned toward him, grinning as well.

226

"Then, by the power vested in me by God and the state of New York, I now pronounce you husband and wife. John, you may NOW kiss your bride," the minister said smiling. Trip let go of John's shoulder.

"Easy, Tiger," Jessica said with a coy smile on her face. "You're a gunshot victim. You don't want to hurt yourself."

"I'll chance it," John said as he leaned in to kiss her. Everyone started clapping. They broke the kiss, smiling.

"May I now present to you, Mr. and Mrs. John Fowler," the minister said. John had a thought.

"Are you ok with that?" he asked. Jessica turned to him and smiled.

"I keep telling you I'm a southern girl, John. What would my parents say if I didn't take your last name?" she asked. John shook his head.

"Really?" he asked. Jessica made a sign of crossing her heart. Arthur and Madeline came up to hug her, and John let it go as he joined in the celebration with his friends.

Chapter 100

A few hours later the newly married John and Jessica Fowler arrived at the cemetery where Sam was buried. John got out of the car and looked it over. Jessica was on her phone talking to someone. John smiled at her, and Jessica put her finger up apologetically to let him know it would be just a minute. John nodded and headed into the cemetery. Earlier, John had begged Trip to let him back on cases and was emphatically told no. John paused for a second and wondered if Jessica was calling his doctor to see how much physical activity he was allowed right now. John laughed out loud at the thought.

John heard the car door open and turned. As he saw Jessica exit the car, what could only be described as a fleet of black SUVs pulled up in the cemetery. John instinctively reached for his gun that wasn't there. He then saw the grin on Jessica's face and quickly realized she was behind this. A couple of Secret Service guys that he recognized were coming toward him. John was pretty sure they were going to pat him down when a voice called out.

"Will you leave that boy alone?" Jeremiah Cosby called out. John smiled as he saw his old friend. The Secret Service agent nearest him appeared to roll his eyes behind his dark sunglasses.

"I dare say you've never had an assignment like him?" John asked the agent. The agent chuckled, nodded, and walked back to the SUV he had come from. John watched as Jeremiah hugged Jessica and then turned toward John. Jeremiah walked over to him, hand extended. John grabbed it and pulled the vice president into a hug. Jeremiah clapped him on the back and whispered into his ear.

"About time, ma'boy. About time." John couldn't agree more. The two men broke the embrace and waited for Jessica to join them. They all three walked toward

Sam's grave. When they reached it, they stood there silent for a few minutes.

Chapter 101

"We miss you, sweetie," Jessica finally said, very quietly. John put his arm around Jessica's shoulders. She continued. "I hope you're proud of us."

"I'ma sorry, ma'dear," Jeremiah began, but stopped.

"She knows what Bruce did wasn't your fault, Jeremiah," Jessica said to him. Jeremiah could only nod. John knew this was one of those times he shouldn't, but he asked anyway.

"Any word on Bruce?" he asked Jeremiah. Jeremiah shook his head.

"He's getting help," Jeremiah began but just shook his head. He was at a loss for words. He just looked at John and shrugged. John nodded. They stood there quietly for several minutes, not saying a word. Jessica walked back to the car and retrieved some flowers from the wedding and placed them on Sam's gravesite. John broke the silence.

"The way we started eight years ago, did you ever think we'd be here?" John asked. Jeremiah laughed out loud, and Jessica shook her head.

"I didn't think we'd last eight weeks after my impromptu interrogation with our first suspect," Jessica said, laughing. "I thought Trip was going to stroke out over that incident!" All three laughed out loud. After a moment, the laughter died. Jessica was rubbing John's arm, thinking. She paused for a second and turned to Jeremiah. "Jeremiah, does John still have that authority? Is he still in charge of the New York taskforce and have authority to take any case he thinks is being overlooked?" Jeremiah nodded, smiling. Jessica turned to John who looked dumbfounded.

"You were reinstated to your former position fully," Jeremiah said, simply. "You still have the authority given you by the FBI and Homeland Security to pursue any case you think might be overlooked. However, you are not cleared to return to work yet. You have at least eight weeks to do whatever you want, ma'boy. Have you thought about writing a book on that first case? I'ma sure it would be a bestseller." John barked a laugh.

"Who would read that?" he asked.

"That other fella wrote one," Jeremiah replied. The two men turned and started walking back to the car and the Secret Service men while Jessica stood there. She looked off to the edge of the woods. She shook her head; she couldn't believe what she was seeing. At the edge of woods was Sam, but it wasn't quite her. Jessica waved, but whoever she saw was gone. Jessica smiled, turned, and walked toward the car. As she passed a tree, there stood Sam leaning against it, grinning. Jessica looked, and no one could see Sam from that angle. Jessica rolled her eyes and shook her head. When she looked back at Sam, Sam squinted her nose at her.

"Home wrecker," she said, still smiling. "I'd hug you, but then you'd have a whole lot of questions to answer from the suit patrol over there. Look, I'm happy for both of you, but there's something I have to tell you. This is it. Do you understand? This is the last time I can talk to you." Jessica nodded. "It's not over, but more importantly, it's not her fault. When it's time, you tell John it's not her fault. Do you understand?" Jessica had never seen Sam so serious. Jessica nodded.

"Why didn't you wave when I saw you a second ago?" Jessica asked. Sam looked very sad.

"That wasn't me," Sam said. Jessica looked very confused. She turned back to where she had seen Sam earlier and then back around. Sam was gone. She looked around and saw John giving her a strange look. She waved and headed toward him with Sam's last words ringing in her ears.

"Tell him it's not her fault." What did that mean?

Chapter 102

Many hours later, John woke with a start for the second morning in a row. He hadn't heard something this time; he was hurting. His arm felt dead. He laid there for a second and then began to chuckle to himself. He looked over beside him and saw what the problem was. Jessica was lying on his arm, and John realized he couldn't feel his fingers.

"The one advantage to being married before," he said to himself quietly. He pulled his arm out from under Jessica with a trick he had learned from his first marriage. As he got up, he noticed Jessica had wormed her way into taking over three-fourths of the bed. John shrugged and wandered into the living room. John scratched his head, not sure what to do. He didn't have to work the next morning; in fact, he was going to have a lot of time to himself until he healed up. Trip had warned him earlier that day that if he kept pushing it, he would keep him out the full six months.

John hadn't wanted to admit to Jessica that walking through the cemetery earlier had about worn him out. He was feeling a little stronger every day, but he knew he still had a ways to go before he was ready to return to work. John found himself looking out the window at the view. Sam had loved the city. That was the only reason he was in New York. John would have gone anywhere for the FBI, but her work brought her here, and he knew what it had meant to her. John chuckled at the irony of it all. He looked down at the street and thought he saw Sam. He shook his head and rubbed the sleep from his eyes. He looked back, and whatever, or whoever, he had seen was gone.

"Bored of me so soon?" he heard behind him. John turned around, and saw Jessica standing.

"No, I was having some pain," John said truthfully. Jessica frowned.

232

"Did we overdo it?" Jessica asked. John shook his head.

"No, I think everything going on today wore me out a little, and honestly, the walk in the cemetery did tire me some, but I'm ok." Jessica stared at John like he was the biggest idiot in the world. John felt like he should know what was going on, and then, it dawned on him.

"Oh--" John began and paused. A grin covered Jessica's face. "Oh," John said again. Jessica was slowly nodding. "Did you mean--" Jessica crossed her arms and leaned against the wall, waiting to hear what would come out of his mouth next. John shook his head and stuck his hands in his pajama's pockets. He kept shaking his head slightly while sticking out his bottom lip. He waved it off like it was nothing. Jessica laughed lightly and turned to head back to the bedroom.

"Should I come with you?" John called after her. Jessica paused midstride and looked up at the ceiling.

"Good grief," she said to herself. "I would hope so," she called back out. John stood there for a minute, nodding, and then decided to go to bed. As he reached the doorway, he had one last question and stopped to ask it.

"Do you want to go away on a honeymoon?" John asked. Jessica didn't answer except for tossing the shirt she was wearing in his face. "We can talk about that tomorrow," he decided. And, that's exactly what they did.

Two Weeks Later
John and Jessica's Apartment

Chapter 103

John brought the freshly homemade pizza into the living room. Upon returning from their honeymoon, Jessica had made the suggestion to invite Trip and Chet over to the apartment. John had agreed. He had asked about including Ron, but Jessica told him this was just for the original team tonight.

After all that had happened over the past few months, he could hardly believe where he was in his life. Trip had asked him about writing a book. John had made a deal with Trip. Trip had agreed to let him work on the old cold cases from home. If he should solve them or get bored, then he would work on a book. John knew there was no chance of that ever happening. Honestly, who would want to read a book about an FBI agent?

John looked at his wife, there was something he was going to have to get used to saying again, and then at his friends, Trip and Chet. Trip was watching John closely. Trip stood up holding his can of soda.

"If I may?" Trip asked. John nodded. "To old friends, old memories, and the new ones we all deserve to have."

"Here, here," Chet added on. Jessica stood up, and John tried not to roll his eyes. She pointed at him.

"Do you want to sleep on the couch tonight?" she asked.

"No, dear," John replied. Trip turned to Chet.

"Isn't it nice to see that even he can be domesticated?" Trip said. John mouthed 'ha-ha'. Jessica smiled and went on.

"To friends we've lost," everyone nodded. "To friends we've saved." Jessica first looked at Chet, then John, and then finally Trip; they all nodded. "And, finally, to moving forward and facing whatever challenges face us," she finished.

"I mean, really, what can't we face?" John asked, his can of soda up in a toasting position. "We've faced our worst and darkest moments, and we've come out of it stronger than ever." Everyone nodded with smiles on their faces. "I can honestly say this, to my friends. May everyone be as lucky to have the ones I have to face their deepest, darkest moments."

"Here, here," they all said together. Jessica leaned back on the couch and smiled.

"You know, I think you three are the closest thing I have to true family," she said. John paused for a second and looked over at her, shock dawning on his face.

"Your parents," he said looking concerned. Jessica gave him an amused look. "I've not met your parents."

"Or my four brothers and sisters," she replied coyly. John nearly choked on his drink.

"You have four brothers and sisters!?" he exclaimed. Jessica smiled, took a sip of her drink, set it down, and looked at him.

"Did you know I've talked to your Mom and Dad numerous times since the wedding?" she asked. Chet and Trip were enjoying this exchange immensely. Jessica looked over at them and grinned.

"Want to see the bomb?" she asked them. They both nodded eagerly. Jessica turned toward John. "I was born and raised in Knoxville, Tennessee." John's mouth dropped. He spoke very softly.

"Then that means . . ." He couldn't finish the sentence. Jessica gladly finished it for him.

"You married the enemy," she replied, her eyes dancing. Chet was utterly confused. Trip turned toward him

"College basketball," he said simply. "You've gotta live there to understand it." Chet just nodded. Jessica took John's hand.

"I told you how I had to pay my own way through college," she said. "My family was upset with me. I've tried to make up with Mom and Dad, but, well, we're all stubborn. I should probably go visit them and take my new husband with me." John looked pained. "Anyway, that's why I say you three are my family. Heck, if Sam was here, I would include her in that number."

"If Sam was here, it would be quite awkward," John deadpanned. Jessica snorted. "Oh, great," he continued. "I find out she snorts after I marry her." Jessica punched him lightly on the arm.

"You know what I mean," she replied. She leaned back and thought about what Sam had said to her and decided now was as good of a time as any to see if John had seen Sam since the wedding.

Chapter 104

Jessica leaned in close to John to try to whisper without being heard.

"By the way, have you," Jessica looked over at Chet and Trip, blew out a breath, and turned back to John. "You know, seen her?" John looked confused.

"Sam?" he asked. Jessica nodded. John thought for a second and shook his head. "No, not since I was . . . well, whatever it was I was doing, dying?" Jessica nodded and placed her hand on his knee. John put his hand on hers and continued. "She said she loves us both." John looked over at Chet and Trip, expecting some type of comment or for them to look at him like he was crazy. Instead, they both sat there quietly, seeming to understand.

"I told them while you were recovering at your ex-in-laws," Jessica explained.

"And, they don't think we're crazy?" John asked.

"Not any more than usual," Trip deadpanned. John smiled and then looked at Jessica, and there was a wry smile on her face.

"You think it was really her?" she asked quietly. John shrugged.

"I have no idea," he replied. "If it wasn't for her, I literally wouldn't have you guys. I wonder if she knew how this was all going to turn out." John said and took a drink of his soda.

"It wouldn't surprise me at all if she did," Trip replied. "She was a remarkable woman." Everyone nodded and voiced their agreement. Jessica decided to let it go. Something bothered her, but she was sure they would figure it out when the time came. The thought that the promise she and Sam made to each other to watch out for the other one if one of them died wouldn't leave her mind. Was Sam an angel, a ghost, a figment of her and John's imagination? She didn't know.

Jessica didn't even realize she had spaced out with her thinking until John gave her a concerned look. She smiled at John and joined in the conversation. The four friends began to talk about different things, enjoying their meal and the camaraderie.

Outside John's apartment, a young woman stared up through the window at the forms of the four people inside. She reached into her shirt, pulled out a locket that hung from her neck, and opened it. She stared at the image inside. If anyone glanced at her and the image quickly, they might have thought it was a mirror, but on closer inspection, they would have noticed minor differences. The young lady looked at the picture of her mother, Samantha Moore. She then glanced up at the apartment window of the man her mother had later married, John Fowler. She saw the shapes of his friends and his new wife. The young woman closed the locket, took one last glance at the window, and decided tonight was not the time to introduce herself to the man that took her mother away from her father. No, tonight was not the night to introduce herself to the man that had destroyed her family. It would be soon, very soon in fact, but not tonight.

The End . . . For Now.

www.ingramcontent.com/pod-product-compliance
Lightning Source LLC
Chambersburg PA
CBHW071311250626
47159CB00004B/1381

* 9 7 8 0 9 8 5 9 5 1 4 7 4 *